THE FESTIVAL

STEVEN T. THOMAS

A Novella

THE FESTIVAL

STEVEN T. THOMAS

Horror Haven Books
3237 Muir Rd.
Dryden, MI 48428
www.authorsteventhomas.com

This novella is dedicated to anyone who has ever experienced religious trauma in their life.

This is for you.

THE FESTIVAL

The following publication features scenes of intense moments, descriptions of blood and gore, violence in reference to religion and some harsh language. Reader discretion is advised.

PROLOGUE
SATURDAY, AUGUST 17TH

As I awoke, face down in the mud, I noticed the aroma of dirt and grass filling my senses. I blinked my eyes a few times and slowly rose to my feet, ensuring I could keep my balance. As I stood, my head began to pound like a drum, and I noticed my sight blurring at the edges. I sat back down on the ground, and the overwhelming urge to vomit began to fill my entire being; my stomach was twisted into knots, and the feeling of heartburn filled my chest as I could feel bile attempting to make its way up my esophagus. I gagged and retched a few times, spitting up nothing but stomach acid with a tinge of the Tito's I was drinking last night, still in my system.

I observed the forest; a light humming sound was still coming from the speakers on the stage, and fog filled the air. Still, I was unsure if it was natural mist coming from the stage's artificial machines. The lighting rails mounted to the platform's top were hanging precariously along with once meticulously placed streamers and banners wafting in the breeze. The morning sun was peeking through the trees, and the pounding in my head intensified as I looked up. I looked directly at the bright ball of light in the sky.

I reached up and touched my head to try to steady myself and reduce the pain I was feeling, squeezing each side of my head in an attempt to feel better. I could feel that my hair was in shambles in the back, a tangled mess that would take a long time to get back to normal, but a piece of my pink highlights hung straight in front of my eyes. I looked down at myself, observing blood stains on my white tank top, unsure of whose blood it was. I winced at the thought.

I covered my face with the palms of my hands and cried silently, but I'm not sure why; I was the only one left. I leaned backward and let my body fall to the ground, landing the back of my head on something soft. I didn't care much about what it was; I was just happy to have something to rest my banging head on. I closed my eyes and turned my head to my right, placing pressure on the source of the headache. As I did, I re-opened my eyes to discover that I was using someone's body as a makeshift pillow. Upon the realization, vomit crawled up my throat again, and I spewed the rest of my stomach's contents onto the ground and quickly scrambled to my feet.

I looked around and examined the remains of a high-energy music festival; luckily, most attendees could flee, but unfortunately for my friends and myself, we were not. We were trapped here with a sadistic killer, and it seems they achieved what they came here to do: kill as many people as they could without being caught. I should have felt lucky that I survived with nothing more than a migraine, but I couldn't help but feel sorry for everyone else's families; my friends and the other seven bodies that I counted that were still lying on the ground.

I bend down next to Mackenzie, my best friend since elementary school, and run my hand through her long, blonde locks, and sorrow fills my mind. After today, I'll never see her again, speak to her again, and hear her laugh again.

How will I explain this to anyone?

I stood back up and looked around again, looking for any way out. Still, until that point, I couldn't even remember how we managed to get here through the winding, twisted trails of the woods. The throbbing in my head was making it even harder to think. I had to have been passed out for hours, and it made me wonder why I wasn't hearing any sirens and no one had been there yet.

I stumbled over to the stage, limping, trying to remember what may have happened to my leg. I guessed I had twisted my ankle running at some point, but most of the night was a broken mess of memories. I wasn't sure if it was the alcohol consumption or how quickly everything happened. I pulled myself up and looked around; music equipment was strewn all over the platform, and blood droplets painted the floor.

I recognized the humming from the speakers again and realized how much the high-pitched sound bothered my head. I walked over to the speakers and unplugged anything I could find to keep them from making more noise. As I pulled the cables out of the sound system, they cracked with the half-connection they were making. I continued making my way through them until the area was silent.

The quietness of the forest was both welcome and eerie. Even though the sun was coming up, the atmosphere held undertones of unease, and I kept feeling like I was being watched. It was almost like I could feel someone's eyes trained on me, and I looked out into where the crowd stood last night, looking for anything that might point me to why I was feeling the way I was.

I couldn't see anything except trees, dense brush, and fog, slowly dissipating as the air warmed around me. I sat down on the edge of the stage and swung my legs, examining the bodies on the ground, wondering still how the hell I was going to escape the nightmare. I reached into my pocket and pulled out my phone. A new crack ran across the screen, and I remembered I didn't have any signal, which should have been the first sign that something wasn't right when we arrived.

Out of desperation, I unlocked my phone and attempted to dial nine-one-one. As a surprise, the other end of the phone began ringing, but just as it did, my phone screen went black, and the battery gave out, leaving me on my own to figure out how to get out of the hellish landscape that contained my friends' bodies. I didn't have much of a choice.

I hopped down off the stage, and as I landed on the ground, my ankle twisted again, sending sharp pain through my leg. I winced, and my eyes pricked with tears. Still, I leveled myself and began walking to the first path I could see, stepping over the tattered remains of the concertgoers who weren't so lucky.

I stepped onto a dark, winding path, shaded by trees on either side, almost entirely from the sunlight that was getting brighter by the minute. I only walked for about five minutes before I was stopped dead in my tracks. In the distance, I heard a twig snap before me, and I stared down the trail. I attempted to slow my breathing to try to hear anything and everything happening around me, but hearing my heartbeat inside my head made it difficult.

Suddenly, a rustling sound grabbed my attention toward the twig breaking. A figure stepped out of the woods onto the path before me, a little ways ahead but still directly in front of me. They were dressed from head to toe in black and were seemingly staring at me, holding a knife in one of their hands. My heart began pounding out of my chest, and I darted my eyes from side to side, looking for some sort of hiding place. I could no longer control my breathing, and I started to hyperventilate. I placed my hands over my mouth to quiet myself down.

I knew there was no escape, and there was no way I could maneuver myself without making noise and grabbing even more of their attention. With how things were left at the festival grounds, I assumed they didn't intend to leave any survivors. When I thought all was lost, and I was done for, the figure turned on their heels and walked back into the woods.

CHAPTER 1
WEDNESDAY, OCTOBER 4TH

The therapist's office has, over the last couple of months, become my second home; I'm here at least three times a week dealing with PTSD and anxiety. That's at least what she tells me she's diagnosed me with. I'm sick of coming here, but I know I can't deal with these demons inside my mind by myself, and it's nice to get out of the house for a little while. It allows me to avoid my mother being up my ass all the time as if I'm going to be murdered as soon as I step out the front door. She seems to think that someone will be coming after me with a thirst for blood simply for surviving what's been dubbed "the festival massacre" by the media.

That's not the case; if someone were to come after me, I like to think that they would have already. It makes me feel better to think of it like that. There's another part of my mind that tells me someone is out there, watching my every move, waiting for their chance to pounce--to finish the job.

"Jessica," a sweet voice says from the hallway.

I pull back as far as I can on the rubber band around my wrist and snap it against my skin as hard as possible. It's a coping mechanism I'd discovered. Even though my therapist says it's unhealthy, I find it better than turning to alcohol or drugs--I need something to take my mind off of what happened, especially when I'm forced to re-live it a few times every week.

SNAP.

Emma Carter has been my therapist for the last several weeks after the first two decided they couldn't handle me. I'll admit I was at my worst for the first month after the massacre, and I couldn't even stand to be within my own body for a while. I felt disgusting and undeserving of the life I still had after ten people were killed during the music festival--I still do, just a little bit. The two of us haven't even discussed the festival in great detail. Emma knows what happened, as does half the town, but she hasn't asked me to dive any deeper. She warned me at our last session two days ago that today would be the day, and I would dread every second.

SNAP.

Hesitantly, I stand up and head to the hallway, keeping my head down and not looking at Emma. My heart is pounding out of my chest, and my hands are beginning to shake. I don't want to do this; I don't want to share every detail of what happened that night, which was supposed to be full of laughter and entertainment. A night that turned deadly and full of bloodshed.

Emma steps foot inside her office, and I hang back, standing in the doorway and leaning my shoulder against the doorframe. I inspect the interior as though someone is waiting inside to come after me. As expected, it's dingy, but it doesn't feel dirty. It's dark inside yet inviting. Soft, meditative music plays on low, and the room smells lavender. It's both inviting and calming, yet eerie and unsettling at the same time.

SNAP.

Emma turns and stares at me.

"Didn't we talk about that?" She asks, her sweet, low voice reminding me of our conversation. One eyebrow is slightly raised, and a smirk tugs at the corners of her mouth.

"You talked," I replied, still looking at the floor. Clearly, I didn't listen."

Emma waves me inside, but as I step forward, I hesitate briefly, considering turning around and never returning to this place. I inhale deeply, taking in the lavender scent, hoping it calms my mind even slightly. I don't subscribe to the essential oils belief system, though. Finally, I step inside the room and examine the seating options; an old suede chair sits in the corner alongside a newer, plush-looking couch.

"You know the drill," Emma says.

"I sure do," I respond.

As always, I choose the couch; it's much more comfortable than the chair and allows me to lie down if need be, which happens more often than not. Our sessions are longer than usual, and I usually end up being here for about two hours. I can't imagine sitting in that seventies-style chair for that long, and sometimes, it feels good to be horizontal. At the same time, I discuss my problems with Emma.

SNAP.

Emma strides over to the door and closes it, but today, she does something out of the ordinary, and I don't think that she realizes that I noticed that she clicked the deadbolt on the door. I keep quiet because maybe it's something, maybe it's nothing. It could be me being paranoid, as I tend to be lately.

She walks back to her chair in the corner next to her laptop and takes a seat as she turns on a page on her yellow legal pad, which she uses to take notes during our sessions. Then she looks up at me. Crossing her legs and tapping her pen on the paper pad, she expects me to initiate the conversation, but I know she knows I won't. I always wait for her to begin.

"Jessica," she starts, her soft voice floating through the air in the room, "whenever you're ready. You already know what I want you to talk about."

Inhale. Exhale.

I'm not ready for this.

SNAP.

***

FRIDAY, AUGUST 16TH

The sunset disappeared behind the trees, and all the lights above the stage went out as they did. Scattered screams could be heard among the crowd, along with indistinct conversation and excitement in the darkness. All the glow bracelets among the crowd were clearly visible, illuminating little bits and pieces of the people eagerly awaiting the first band to come out on stage.

The annual Metal Apocalypse Festival was a highly anticipated event each year, hosting twenty different metal bands throughout two nights. Mackenzie, Adam, Joe, and I had all purchased our tickets months in advance, so to say we were excited was an understatement. Along with many others, we set up camp nearby to stay on the festival grounds for the duration of the shows.

From the platform in front of us, the speakers crackled and screamed feedback as the lights came back above the stage. Five first band members walked out, waving at the crowd as they made their grand entrance. Sounds of screaming and cheering filled the forest, and with an abrupt guitar strum, they began their first song. Mackenzie bumps me on the arm and holds out a shot of Tito's, which I took with excitement, cracked open, and dumped down my throat in one swift gulp.

The aroma of sweaty bodies and marijuana filled the air as the band continued their set. Any average person would stray from these things. Still, we were in heaven, enjoying ourselves and having a good time without a care. A guy next to me, headbanging like his life depended on it, without missing a beat, reached over and held out a joint, offering up a couple puffs. I shrugged and hit it, handing it directly back to him afterward. I coughed my lungs out, and the mixture of weed with the alcohol hit my bloodstream seemingly right away.

Around me, the world began to spin, and I was in a state where I didn't care about anything. I looked over and observed my friends enjoying every minute of the show along with myself. I still had some control over my actions, and I wasn't entirely out of my mind, but I was definitely under the influence.

As the band was completing their set and running through their last song, the singer shouted into the microphone as loudly as he could in a deep growl, causing the speakers to crackle.

"This is our last song of the night, so open up this pit," he screamed.

Being only a few rows back from the stage, the people directly in front of us swiftly began running and jumping, banging into one another. I watched as a few people got picked up and thrown on top of the crowd and began surfing across others on their backs, ultimately getting dropped on the ground. The mosh pit opened up even further and spread into my friends. Before I knew it, they had disappeared into a sea of other humans, and I couldn't find them.

I don't know if it was the weed, the alcohol, or a combination of both; maybe it was my own paranoia, but I began to panic as I realized I was alone. Frantically, I started looking around, trying to find them; part of me wanted to protect them from getting hurt in the pit, and the other didn't want to be alone.

As I searched for them, someone got knocked into me, and before I knew it, I was flat on my back on the ground. I hit my head against the hard floor of the forest and lay for a moment, staring up at the dark star-filled sky. I watched as beams of light danced in my vision so severely that I had to blink several times to get them to leave my sight.

Sitting up, attempting to regain my bearings, I kept myself sitting on the ground, looking around for any sign of my friends to the best of my abilities. I looked dead ahead into the pit and watched as people intermittently fell to the ground and jumped right back up. The mosh pit condensed and became much smaller than it had started, and as I looked into the middle, a hooded figure dressed in all black turned and stared at me. I rubbed my eyes, thinking I was hallucinating. Then, a flash of light reflected in my eyes as the mysterious person showed me a blood-stained knife, then disappeared into the ground.

Inspecting further, I could just barely make out the face of someone lying on the ground, eyes wide, blood running down their face, seemingly staring at me. They were illuminated momentarily by the spotlight above the stage as it panned across the crowd.

The sight made me scream at the top of my lungs, but the music was so loud that no one could hear me.

CHAPTER TWO
WEDNESDAY, OCTOBER 4TH

I look over toward Emma, who is scribbling notes on her legal pad. She's not making eye contact with me but feverishly writes in her notebook. I examine her body language; her shoulders are lifted slightly, almost like she's carrying some baggage that no one knows about. She looks tense in the way she is writing things down, and her knuckles look white from the grip she has on her pencil.

"How did that make you feel?" She asks suddenly, a smile tugging on the corners of her mouth.

"Really?" I ask in a sarcastic tone. "You're going to be cliché?"

She peers up at me with searching eyes as she attempts to read my body language.

"How did that make you feel?" I repeat, mockingly, "How do you think it made me feel?" The question spills from my mouth more aggressively than I intended, and I can feel my face flushing red from the embarrassment.

The two of us sit silently for a moment, and Emma nods, making a "hmm" sound. Then, she looks back down and scribbles more notes into her notepad. I reach across to the coffee table in front of me and pick up the Rubik's cube, fiddling with it with no intention of solving it as the silence between us drones on for what feels like an eternity.

"Okay, so you saw what you thought to be a dead body right in front of your eyes. Is that correct?" She asks, almost as if she doesn't believe me.

"No, what I saw was a dead body right in front of my eyes; not what I thought I saw, but what I know I saw," I state, boring into her with my eyes.

"Well, you did say you were under the influence of drugs and alcohol," she accuses.

It wasn't that bad.

"The same dead body was on the ground when I woke up and had sobered up, so don't be accusing me of hallucinating everything. There were ten dead bodies when I woke up; three of those were my friends. I know what I saw," I say, sitting more upright and confidently.

I set the Rubik's cube back on the coffee table and began fiddling with the rubber band on my wrist again. I consider snapping it again, but that would fuel Emma's feverish note-taking.

SNAP.

Habit.

She peers up at me again with disapproving eyes and stares in my direction for a minute. The look she's giving me is the same look previous therapists had given me right before they told me they couldn't see me anymore, essentially calling me a lost cause. I don't try to be uncooperative; it just happens. I promised myself I wouldn't be like that with Emma, and now, it seems like she's about to drop me as a patient, too. I may be a lost cause.

"If we are going to make this work, Jessica, you need to trust me, be open, and quit being so standoffish. I allowed you to have our first ten sessions without actually talking about the festival because I thought that might help, but as soon as I ask you to talk about the events, you're acting the same way your previous therapists presented you:" Emma says, "Please work with me."

"I'm trying," I say, snapping my wrist again.

"We need to work on that, too," Emma states.

"I know," I reply, looking at the floor.

I close my eyes and inhale deeply, noticing that the room no longer smells like Lavender but more musty, as if no one had cracked the door in a few months. I look at the essential oil diffuser and notice that steam is no longer wafting into the air.

"Would you mind starting that up again?" I request, pointing at the diffuser on the shelf across from me.

"Are you ready to continue?" Emma asks as she stands up to refill the bottle of water she has in her hand.

"Yes," I confirm.

She waves her hand in my direction as if to say, "Whenever you're ready." Staring across the room, I focus on every drop of essential oil as it falls and splashes into the water. I swing my legs up on the couch and get comfortable, situating a throw pillow just right underneath my head and neck, and stare at the ceiling.

***

FRIDAY, AUGUST 16TH

I continued screaming at the top of my lungs, but no one seemed to hear me. The song's final chord from the band playing on stage ripped through the air. It faded out, overtaken by scattered screaming and cheering from the crowd. Suddenly, a hand reached down and hooked underneath my armpit, pulling me to my feet. I looked over to find Mackenzie and Adam standing beside me as I regained my bearings.

"You good?" Mackenzie asked.

"I'm fine," I confirm, wiping the dust off my pants.

I peered into the middle of the crowd and attempted to spot the dead body I had just seen, but everyone was packed together so tightly that it was difficult to spot. My eyes were welling up with tears. I looked away from Mackenzie and Adam to hide it from them, but just then, screaming ripped through the forest over the indistinct chatter.

The three of us whipped our heads around and stared toward the screaming, and the crowd began to dissipate quickly. As everyone cleared the area, the man's body started coming into view. The dirt on the ground underneath him had turned to mud as the blood spewing from his wounds soaked into the earth. We looked on in horror, and as everyone else returned to their campsites, we locked ourselves down. It felt like I couldn't move my legs, and fear kept me in place.

Joe caught up with us, and it seemed like he had reappeared from the thin air.

"What is going on? I had to fight my way back over here against the crowd," he panted as he tried to catch his breath.

I lifted my arm and pointed to the body on the ground, unable to speak. The words were in my head, but it felt like my brain wasn't communicating correctly with my voice box to let them come out of my mouth.

"Holy hell," Joe yelled, running to the man's side and checking his pulse.

Joe was an EMT and a good one at that. The three of us continued to observe as he searched for a pulse, then hung his head and looked back up at us. The look in his eyes told me that my suspicions were confirmed: the man was dead. There was no more hiding my tears; I wept for him and for his family, who would soon be receiving the news that their relative was dead. I didn't know who he was, but I still grieved for him.

"I saw him," I blurted out again, my mouth spewing the words before my brain could catch up to tell me to keep it shut.

"You saw who?" Mackenzie asked, placing a hand on my shoulder.

"I saw the murderer," I confirmed.

I'll never forget the look of terror on my friend's face as I described the person responsible for the man's death. Although I couldn't catch much detail, I could explain enough that we had something to go off of, something to use and keep our eyes peeled for. I felt an overwhelming urge to warn everyone else at the festival, but there were thousands of people. How could I be sure that everyone knew what to look for?

The indistinct conversation, chatter, and screaming from the crowd in the background seemed to fade out, and a light humming sound filled my head. Frantically, I looked around, attempting to find the source of the noise to make sure I wasn't losing my mind and experiencing an auditory hallucination. The world started spinning around me again as the hit of marijuana made an abrupt appearance again, and I had to reach out and grab onto Mackenzie to steady myself.

Realizing the speakers continued to hum, I had an idea. If I could make my way to the stage, grab a microphone, and make an announcement, I could save everyone there that night. It was almost as if Adam realized the same thing because he tilted his head in the direction of the stage and looked over at me. We had a telepathic conversation and fully understood one another at that moment.

Before I could process or come up with a plan, Adam broke into a full-on sprint toward the platform, heaving himself up over the edge and scrambling to his feet, frantically looking around for a microphone. Finally, he found one and turned it on. The speakers squealed a horrible high-pitched sound that echoed around the forest. For the first time that night, the festival grounds fell silent. I looked around and observed as some people covered their ears and others turned their attention to the stage.

Suddenly, Adam had become the center of attention, with all attendees staring back at him. I watched as he began sweating bullets; he didn't like having all eyes on him.

"Hi everyone," he announced, his voice shaking with nerves, "umm."

Adam wasn't quite sure how to announce that there was a murderer on the loose.

"My friend here, Jessica, she, umm," he started, then suddenly pointed at the ground where the man's corpse lay.

"Dead," he announced.

Suddenly, someone from the back of the crowd near one of the campsites shouted out, "Did she see how he died?"

Adam couldn't muster the words and only nodded in response. I could feel my face flushing out of embarrassment for him. I examined the crowd, as many stood in stunned silence, staring, judging my friend. I ran over to the stage, pulled myself up next to him, and grabbed the microphone.

Oh shit, now they're staring at me.

From behind the people, now all staring at me in silence, I could hear a girl screaming and sobbing but couldn't see her. Her words were unintelligible at first until she emerged from the crowd of attendees standing around. Pushing her way through, she knocked a couple of people over until she was out in the middle of the festival grounds.

"Mark," she yelled, "where's Mark?"

Adam looked at me, and I looked at him, and I just knew we were both thinking the same thing: the dead guy on the ground was Mark. I pulled the microphone up in front of my mouth and froze momentarily. Time seemed to stand still, and I didn't want to be the one to tell her that Mark was dead, let alone tell her that I observed the moment he died.

"Is this Mark?" I asked into the microphone as I pointed at the corpse on the ground, wincing as I awaited her response.

The girl ran over to the body lying on the ground and began sobbing harder. She kneeled down next to the mangled remains of her friend and cried over his body.

"Mark, no," she sobbed, "Mark."

Her howls resonated through the trees, and as if the forest hadn't fallen silent enough, it felt like it had become even quieter.

"I'm sorry," I said into the microphone, my sincere voice echoing through the landscape. She looked up at me, confused, as tears continued to fall down her cheeks.

"H-How?" She asked quietly.

I looked up, and I felt terrible ignoring her question, but the truth of the matter was I didn't know. I didn't know precisely how Mark died. I didn't know the extent of his injuries, and I didn't see the act happen. I was only an innocent bystander in the aftermath. All I knew was I wasn't leaving here until we figured out who was responsible.

Just then, in the distance, I could, just barely in the darkness, make out a figure standing just past the treeline watching us. I stopped, and my hand fell to my side unintentionally. The sight caught me off guard.

"Who did this?" The mystery girl wailed.

As she did, and as I was about to point out the figure standing in the woods, they took off running; evidently, they knew I had spotted them. I watched as they ran around the perimeter of the trees. I dropped the microphone and took off running. I don't know what had gotten into me, but I knew I was putting myself at risk by chasing after them. All my mind was telling me to do was to run after them. Adrenaline was pumping through my body faster than I could process what was happening around me. Still, I could feel the stares of the people as I chased a figure that only I had seen.

"There!" I yelled as I pointed into the distance, seemingly at nothing.

Running as fast as I could, I jumped over obstacles as I could see them, pulling out my phone mid-sprint to turn on my flashlight so I could have some light away from the illumination of the stage. I'd thought I had lost the person when they suddenly flashed back into my line of sight. Behind me, I could hear fearful chatter scattered among the crowd, but I kept running, keeping pace with who I believed to be the killer.

They ran behind the stage, and I continued to chase after them. I reached the backstage area, where instruments and other musical equipment were scattered all over the ground. None of us observed any bands or stagehands leaving the area. I scanned the area and thought I had lost the person, but a sudden movement caught the edge of my vision as I watched them jump onto the stage.

I took off in a full sprint again and followed, jumping on top of the stage. Adam was still standing where I had left him, looking out into the distance where I'd first seen the figure in the woods. I pulled myself back onto the platform and watched helplessly as the person stalked behind Adam. The entire crowd, including Mackenzie and Joe, had their eyes trained on the woods.

The person turned around, almost as if to taunt me. The only thing I could do was watch in fear as I knew what was coming. As I attempted to take off running again, the person pulled their arm back, and a slight glimmer blinded me momentarily. I rubbed my eyes, and the next thing I knew, Adam was screaming at the top of his lungs. From behind, I watched as blood spilled onto the ground in front of him. I found the courage to charge at the person again, but before I could reach them, they exited the stage right. Their knife clattered to the ground, and before I knew it, the person was gone. The crowd turned around, observing the stage. Adam fell to his knees, then fell forward, face-planting onto the floor. At the same time, a spotlight above me shone down and illuminated me, making it difficult to see the crowd. I could only imagine the looks of terror on the people's faces as I was the only one left, standing behind him as he died in front of my eyes.

CHAPTER THREE
WEDNESDAY, OCTOBER 4TH

"Hmm, interesting," Emma said, her judgmental eyes dull into me, searching my soul for answers.

The overall atmosphere in the room had shifted in the last few minutes while I was giving her the rundown of what had happened that night. It feels more tense, even with the diffuser running at full blast and the scent of lavender filling my senses, even more than it was before. I can feel my body sinking into the worn-down couch, and it's comfortable overall, but I can't shake this feeling that something is wrong. I close my eyes and breathe deeply, attempting to calm my muscles.

"What's interesting?" I ask.

"Oh, oh nothing," Emma's sweet voice rings through the air, but her tone does not match the look on her face.

She scribbles something down into her notepad.

"No, what? If you have something to say, say it," I demand, my voice shaking and my words becoming more aggressive.

She sets her pen down on top of the notepad and crosses her legs, staring at me. The overwhelming urge to scream is radiating through my body. I don't even know where this aggression is coming from, but one thing I do know is that I hate it when someone has something to say and they won't say it.

"So, let me ask you this," Emma starts as her eyes seem to be judging me even more, "I just want to clarify. No one except you saw Adam get stabbed and die, right?"

I know where this is headed.

"That's right," I confirm, steadying my tone.

"Not a single person among thousands saw this happen," she repeats.

"From what I could tell, I was the only person who observed it happening."

Emma nods, then picks up her pen, scribbling another note, and I turn my head back and stare at the ceiling. I'm attempting to remember what happened next; the whole night is a blur; everything happened so fast that it is challenging to piece everything together and keep everything in order.

Setting her pen down, Emma swivels in her chair and faces the wall away from me. She clicks around on her computer until a whirring sound fills the air. A piece of paper pops out of her printer and floats to the ground. She bends down and picks it up, handing it to me.

"While you tell me what happened next, I'd like you to complete this questionnaire. It will help me understand things better so that I can help you effectively," she states, holding the piece of paper out toward me.

When I don't get up, she does and crosses the room to hand it to me along with a pen. The look on her face is an almost forced smile. It's like she's trying to be friendly but struggling with it. Her teeth are slightly behind her lips, and her eyes are wide. She looks almost crazed. I look down at the paper and read the first question:

Do you ever drive somewhere and then have no recollection of the trip?

The answer options are a simple yes or no, with some changing it up and asking about the percentage of the time someone experiences a particular event. I glance up at Emma, and she's writing down more notes, and I quickly look down. Before answering anything, I read the questions thoroughly to ensure I understand what they're asking. At first, I was still determining what this was supposed to help with. Still, the survey she had me filling out was the DES-II questionnaire--I remember learning about it in my Introduction to Psychology class.

"Are you ready to continue?" Emma asks, looking up at me with kind eyes.

I'm unsure what's more degrading: having therapists give up on me or having one who's trying to sneakily diagnose me with Dissociative Identity Disorder. I reach for the rubber band on my wrist.

SNAP.

Emma thinks I'm the killer.

"Sure," I reply, ensuring I answer the questions so that the results don't point the finger at me.

***

FRIDAY, AUGUST 16TH

The spotlight shifted positions and moved over to the crowd, panning across. I could see the horrified look on the onlooker's faces. I looked down and scanned for Mackenzie and Joe. Mackenzie had her hands over her mouth, and Joe stood utterly still, mouth agape as she stared back at me. I shook my head to convince them that I didn't kill Adam.

Suddenly, the crowd began to scream again, and more people started running through the festival grounds. I watched as attendees pushed one another over in an attempt to escape down one of the various trails leading out of the forest. I watched as multiple people got knocked to the ground and trampled by the crowd. They were running from who they thought was the killer and, in their attempt, became murderers themselves. Before I could process everything that had happened over the previous few minutes, the forest fell silent, and only scattered screams could be heard in the distance.

Only some people left, though. Some were left behind either unintentionally or by choice. They were still staring at me but weren't running out of fear as many of the others did. Of course, Mackenzie and Joe didn't leave me, either. None of us moved a muscle, not even to check on Adam. Our eyes moved in tandem from one person to the next as if we weren't sure what to do next. The three of us and four others stood around, and I finally found the nerve to move and jump off the stage.

I slowly inched closer to my friends, half expecting them to back away from me out of fear, but they didn't. When I was within arm's length, Mackenzie reached out, grabbed me, and pulled me into her close, holding my head to her chest and squeezing me so hard that I felt the air leave my lungs. As she let me go, I noticed the other four that hung around had begun walking closer to us. Maybe the hug from Mackenzie told them what they needed to know; that I wasn't a threat.

I already felt desensitized to death at that point. I looked around the grounds and noticed that two more dead bodies were lying on the ground. I assumed that they had been trampled in the onslaught of others attempting to escape. It didn't phase me any, which was a strange feeling overall. At this point, the others were right next to us, but they didn't say a word; they just stared at me as I sized them up, trying to figure them out.

"I'm not a killer," I blurted out unintentionally.

There goes my mouth moving quicker than my brain again.

The group looked at one another, almost as if they were having a conversation without speaking.

"We didn't think you were," a girl with sandy blonde, mid-length hair said with a comforting smile.

"We saw whoever, running through the woods; we saw who you were chasing," one of the boys confirmed.

"Why didn't you all run like everyone else?" I inquired.

"We decided as a group to help you catch the person. We didn't know if you all would stick around. Still, when we saw you three staying in place, not running away like everyone else did, we figured we could offer some assistance," the sandy-haired girl said, "my name is Brielle; this is Jordan," she introduced as she held out a hand.

"It's Jessica. It's nice to meet you guys," I said as I held out my hand and returned a handshake, "even under the circumstances."

I looked over at the other girl and guy with them, who had stood still as statues and didn't say anything. I raised a hand in salutation, waving at them. They waved back, although they looked a little more reserved in their greeting toward me.

"So," Brielle said, a little more animated than I thought she should be, "what's the plan?"

I looked to Mackenzie and Joe for some sort of advice, but they both shrugged their shoulders. Everything had happened so quickly that we hadn't had much time to process it or even consider our plan. I wished that guy with the joint was standing next to me. My high felt like it was already wearing off, and I wanted to be a little more chill and clear my mind so I could think.

"We should build a giant fire, considering we have little light. Unless someone knows how to work those," I suggest as I point to the lights above the stage.

We all glared at one another, expecting someone to chime in and say they did, but none of us accepted the offer. We gathered as much wood as possible, staying in groups of four and three, picking up every dead branch we could, and piled it all in the center of the festival grounds.

It took us about twenty minutes to build a giant bonfire that stood about six to seven feet tall. Brielle dug a lighter out of her pocket. She lit the dried leaves we placed underneath the wood pile, and they caught almost instantly, sending flames upward and spreading through the sticks and twigs. The heat was immense and forced us to back away and keep our distance, but it worked as we had hoped, lighting up most of the perimeter. At least that way, we could see if someone was standing at the tree line watching us.

"So, what are your names?" I asked the other two if we still needed to meet officially. They remained quiet and said little except a word here and there.

"Bryan and Kaylee," the guy said. His voice was more profound than his face suggested it would be. Kaylee didn't say anything; she just shot a forced smile in my direction. They didn't want to stay and were forced to by Brielle and Jordan; I was okay with that; we needed all the help we could get.

The only reason I stuck around and didn't run was how I was perceived--as a killer. The way that person cut and ran with Adam left me there to take the blame. I felt an overwhelming sense of rage run through my body, and I couldn't think of anything other than getting payback for them- whoever they were. If I knew then what I know now, I'd have left and taken Mackenzie and Joe with me, never to return to the forest. Then again, I could be in a much different predicament, like possibly being forced to stand trial for a murder that I didn't commit.

After a while, it suddenly felt like we all had known one another for years. The air was still, and the fire was roaring--it felt like we were all friends enjoying a night out around the bonfire together. It was a welcome break from all of the action, but deep in the pit of my stomach, I knew it wasn't going to last. The person, whoever they were, was laying low, watching us, and I couldn't get past the overwhelming feeling that I was being watched. I couldn't help but repeatedly look over my shoulder and peer back into the woods, my gaze scanning for unusual movement.

Suddenly, a whooshing sound ripped through the air, and a light thud on the ground pulled my attention away from the treeline and back to the group. Brielle let out an ear-piercing wail as she watched both Bryan and Kaylee fall to the ground with a single arrow sticking through both their heads, their eyes still wide open.

Two birds, one stone, I thought.

I scrambled to my feet and ran around the other side of the massive bonfire as I assessed what direction the arrow more than likely came from. The light from the fire illuminated the edge of the forest, and I watched as the flash of a black robe whipped in the distance. I looked back to my friends, and Mackenzie's face donned a horrified expression—almost as if she wasn't sure what to do. She looked like she was secured to the ground, unable to move.

Without another thought, I took off running and could hear Mackenzie screaming behind me.

"Jessica, no," she begged, but I brushed her off.

I could hear footsteps pounding behind me, and I glanced back to find Joe and Jordan chasing after me. I wasn't sure if they were trying to catch up to stop me or to help, but I continued pushing forward. The figure seemingly disappeared, and though I couldn't see anything, I kept moving forward, hoping to cut the person off in the woods. Having Jordan and Joe there as backup would be helpful if I corner the mysterious figure.

I glanced back again, and the two boys were a good thirty to forty feet behind me. I considered hanging back and allowing them the opportunity to catch up. Instead, I crashed into the woods and immediately heard the crunch of old, dried leaves underneath my feet. All of a sudden, out of nowhere, I am clotheslined. Before I knew it, I was lying flat on my back with the uncomfortable earth underneath me. I slammed down so hard that it knocked the breath out of me, and I had to take a moment to catch it.

I didn't see what I ran into, but to my right, I heard leaves rustling, heavy footsteps retreating from the area, and a distant evil laugh echoed around me. My vision blurred slightly, and I was having difficulty catching my breath, though, with every attempt, it became easier. I began having difficulty forcing my eyes to stay open until I gave in to them and closed them voluntarily. Like when you've had too much to drink, the world around me continued to spin, even with my eyes shut tightly.

I felt Jordan and Joe come up from behind and grab onto me, but I was already slipping further and further until the world went black.

CHAPTER FOUR
WEDNESDAY, OCTOBER 4TH

Handing the questionnaire back to Emma, she quickly scans it, and I observe as her eyes track back and forth across the paper. She glances up at me with questioning eyes, then looks back down, reviewing the survey again.

"So what happened next?" she asked. Her voice had a slight edge to it now, one that I couldn't quite pinpoint.

"I don't really know. I blacked out. I'm completely unaware of what happened while I was out." My reply is harsh and cold. Admittedly, I'm a little offended by the form she just made me fill out and the silent accusation that I was, somehow, the killer that night.

Emma's eyes narrowed as she finished scanning the paper in her hand, and she set it down on her desk with a light slam. It was unintentional, but she may have caught on to what I did while answering the questions. How she looks at me tells me a story from beginning to end, and I have to force back a devious smile that tugs at the corners of my mouth.

"Did you answer these questions truthfully?" She asks while pointing at the paper.

She looks down at her notepad and feverishly begins taking notes. The scratching of the pen on paper is starting to get on my nerves, and the silent judging is getting under my skin. Therapists aren't supposed to judge their patients, but I can tell that this one does. At least she hasn't dropped me and deemed me a lost cause yet.

"Nope," I reply. My voice bounces with excitement as I admit it to her.

Emma looks at me again with one arched eyebrow, questioning my response.

"Why not?" The questioning tone of her voice takes on a sweeter delivery again.

I knew what that questionnaire was, and I wasn't about to let her section me into a category. I also wasn't going to give her the satisfaction of turning me into the villain of my story or sending me to a padded room. I don't need a grippy sock vacation; I'm not a danger to myself or others. Therefore, if I half-assed my way through the questions, I could show her I was entirely in control of myself and my personality.

"Because I know what the DES-II questionnaire is, and I'm not crazy--" I begin to announce before being cut off.

"I'm not implying that you are; I'm just doing my job," Emma says harshly.

"No, what you're trying to do is implicate me for the murders as a result of having DID." A look falls over my expression that says that I just caught her in a lie.

"I'm not--" she starts, but I cut her off this time.

"Stop," I demand as I rise to my feet, "I'm not an idiot. Stop treating me like I'm stupid."

"Jessica, I need you to sit down." Her demeanor completely changed in an instant, and she rose to her feet as if to challenge me.

Her shoulders are tensed up, and her breathing becomes erratic. I would think that a therapist of all people would have better control over their emotions, but this one is different. There is something wildly dissimilar to the other therapists I've seen in the past few months. Her typically starburst hazel eyes turn dark as she stares me down, almost as if she is willing me to sit back on the couch with her mind. I watch her body shake with anger ever so slightly, and I wonder if she's about to lunge at me. I anticipate the worst, expecting her to tackle me to the ground with a syringe of a sedative in her hand, ready to plunge it into my skin.

She doesn't.

Instead, her body suddenly relaxes, as if she's realized that she's giving something away about herself. Her breathing slows, her body stabilizes, and she slowly lowers herself back down onto her chair, but she keeps her eyes trained on me. Maybe she's expecting me to pull something over on her. She waves her hand in that welcoming way, inviting me to sit back down.

"I just need you to cooperate with me, Jessica," Emma states as she exhales one last relaxing breath.

"I am cooperating with you, but you don't want to listen to me. Instead, you'd rather throw wild accusations in my direction. I'm telling you, it wasn't me. I did not do this. I--I--"

I couldn't kill my best friends, which is what I want to say, but the words get caught in my throat.

Emma writes another note into her legal pad and looks back at me.

"I think I know what we need to do." Her calming personality is back. Maybe she's the one with DID with mood swings like that. "Can you spare a couple of extra hours with me today? I'm going to clear my schedule."

I look in her direction but don't utter a single word. I don't know what she meant by what she said, and I don't want to know. I can't think of any good excuses for my inability to stick around. My mind is racing a million miles per second, and that is the first thing that comes to mind.

"I can make that work," I confirm, shutting my eyes tightly and mentally beating myself up for the answer I gave.

"Good." Emma makes direct eye contact with me again, and her eyes darken again. "Please continue."

****

SATURDAY, AUGUST 17TH

I coughed and sputtered as the world began awakening around me again. Everything was blurry but quickly came back into focus. Looking up, I started to recognize the faces staring back down at me. Brielle, Jordan, Joe, and Mackenzie were standing in a circle above me, and I attempted to lift my head, but then I heard the comforting voice of my best friend.

"Stay down, Jess," Mackenzie said, soothing my ears softly.

"Holy hell," I whispered.

Brielle had her arm outstretched toward me as I approached more and more with each passing second. She was holding a water bottle out for me, and she had a worried smile on her face.

"We thought we lost you," she said, "you had a hell of a spill."

They think I fell, but I didn't fall simply out of clumsiness; someone clotheslined me. The same someone who killed Mark, Adam, Bryan, and Kaylee. It was the same someone who had terrorized us for the last few hours, though I wasn't entirely sure that hours had passed. I may have only been unconscious for a few minutes. I sit up again slowly as I take the water bottle and open the lid, pressing it to my lips to take a sip.

Mackenzie placed a hand on my back to help me up, and the world around me started to spin again, but lightly.

"What happened out there?" Jordan asked. "One moment, you were right before us; the next, you disappeared into the darkness, and we found you on the ground."

It didn't take long for me to blurt out the words and explain that I hadn't experienced a simple slip and fall but that someone had been standing there in the dark, waiting for me to show up to ensure I ended up on my back. My only question was why they hadn't ended me right then and there; they could have cut and run before Jordan and Joe even made it to me.

The two boys jerked their heads around and stared into the woods as if they could see anything past the forest's edge. Mackenzie looked down at me in sheer terror as she realized that I was right next to the person responsible for six dead bodies, either personally or by extension. My face didn't return the fear in her eyes. I kept my expression stoic as I stared back at her as if nothing through that night affected me.

I slowly got back onto my feet, and all four held a different part of my body to keep me as steady as I did. I wobbled a little bit, then was able to regain my bearings. I sipped the water again and looked around, noticing the fire was dying slightly. I walked over and started grabbing extra wood by the armful we hadn't added to the fire earlier, just in case we needed extra.

"Jess, are you sure you should be doing that?" Brielle asked as she ran to my side and attempted to take the wood from me.

Like a child about to get their favorite toy taken away from them, I jerked my arms out of her reach. I continued walking back and forth between the fire and the small woodpile until the fire was sufficiently built back up in my eyes. I wasn't one to ever ask for help, so for Brielle to assume I needed or wanted it offended me a bit. I dropped the thought because she didn't know me, and I decided we needed to keep our alliance.

Only five of us remained, and it was only a matter of time before another one was picked off. It seemed there was nothing we could do to stop it. This person was too strong, too swift, and too sneaky. We had yet to begin coming up with a plan. Still, I felt like we needed to come up with some sort of booby traps to surround the area to either alert us or stop someone from coming anywhere near.

I couldn't speak for the other two. Still, I know myself, Mackenzie, and Joe didn't know the first thing about using only what nature provides to build any trap, so the idea. At the same time, it flashed through my mind, fell by the wayside before I could fully consider making the suggestion. Suddenly, another thought crossed my mind, and I realized I didn't know the time.

"Who has the time?" I asked out loud, taking everyone around me off guard.

Jordan raised his wrist and looked at his watch, "1:13 AM. Why?"

"Just wondering," I replied.

I wondered if daybreak would give us the advantage we needed. Still, by then, the person responsible for the mess would be long gone. I felt that if we waited that long to take action, we would all be dead. I shivered at the thought.

Looking up at everyone and coming out of my stupor, where I'd been keeping myself primarily within my own thoughts, I noticed I was receiving some strange looks from Brielle and Jordan, almost as if they were once again blaming me for all of this happening. It was weird that every time something happened, no one else saw anything; no one except for me. Why was I the only one? It definitely made me look bad to the rest of the group. I finally decided to share my thoughts with the rest of them.

"I say we just hunker down until the sun begins rising again," I said, and the rest of the group looked at me like I was nuts.

"Just hang out and let this psychopath pick us off one at a time?" Joe asked, almost accusingly.

"What else do you think we could do?" I posed the question as if I was looking to him for an answer. "We can barely see out there, at least with the sunrise. It opens the woods, and we can see what might be out there."

"Yeah, and by then, the person is gone. Then what do we do?" Brielle asked.

"Then we make a run for it. As fast as we can, we get out of here and report this to the police." I stated.

My eyes wandered over to Joe again; the way he spoke to me a few seconds before lingered in the back of my mind. He was sitting on the ground with a knife and a stick, looking like he was shaving down the end into a sharp point. I hadn't even noticed previously that he was doing it. I was so focused on what we should do that I hadn't seen him.

He placed his finger on the tip of it and pulled it back quickly, but I noticed a small, faint spot of red on the tip of his finger.

Damn.

I sauntered over to Joe and observed what he was doing. The makeshift spear he had crafted looked sharp, and an idea popped into my head. I turned to the rest of the group.

"What if we made a bunch of these and charged into the woods as a group. Five against one are pretty good odds." I suggested. "Unless you guys want to wait until morning, as I mentioned."

A quick scan of the group told me they were nervous to wander deep into the dark woods. Truth be told, I was, too, but Joe and Brielle made good points that we were just sitting ducks if we waited until morning. The only one who seemed to agree was

Jordan—weird based on the previous expressions he had been giving me. The look he gave me told me he was on my side with the idea.

I reached down and grabbed the spear out of Joe's hands.

"Hey," he yelled as he grabbed back for it.

"Can you stay here and make some more?" I asked. "I'm going into the woods to see if I can spot anything."

I am still determining where the sudden bravery came from. The rest of the group looked at me like I was completely nuts, except Jordan. He stepped up and held out his hand to Joe.

"Give me the knife; she needs someone with her. I was an Eagle Scout. I know how to make a spear, " he said.

Joe hesitantly handed the knife over to Jordan, looking at him as if Jordan was about to reach out and stab him as soon as the weapon was in his hands. He didn't.

Joe and I ventured deeper into the darkness until we were at the edge of the woods. The sound of the fire crackling behind us faded away, and the scattered murmurs among the group did the same the further we went. We began walking the perimeter of the woods, keeping close to the campsites, making sure we didn't go too deep into the abyss of trees and vegetation. We moved in silence, at least as much as we could muster, with the sounds of leaves crunching and twigs snapping under each step.

Suddenly, a snapping sound came from our left, deeper into the woods. The closer we listened, the more we realized we heard more than just a branch breaking. We kept our attention on the woods as we zoned in on the sound. It sounded like a woman crying. Even though we could barely see two feet in front of us, we looked at one another, and I could tell we were thinking the same thing.

"Help," cried the voice in the woods, "help me."

"I've seen enough horror movies to know you don't walk toward the sound of the creepy voice," Joe whispered.

I didn't reply. Instead, it felt like an invisible force took me over, and even though my brain was telling me to stay put, my feet wanted to move. I was walking forward into the woods, looking to investigate the voice.

"Jess," Joe said, keeping his voice low.

But I kept moving forward.

When he realized he wouldn't stop me, I could hear his footsteps behind me, keeping very little distance between us.

"Is anyone out there?" The voice asked as it became louder. "Help me."

Then, silence.

We halted our search and listened again for the voice, but nothing came.

We waited.

And waited.

For what felt like an eternity. Suddenly, I felt a tug on the spear in my hand. I gripped it firmly, then felt an even harder tug, but we were deep enough into the woods that I couldn't see a thing in front of my face. Another tug and the weapon slipped from my grasp. I turned to look at Joe and tell him to run, but suddenly, I heard a gagging sound as my head flipped toward him. Coughing and retching began when suddenly I felt liquid spray on my face.

Instinctively, I threw my hands up to wipe off my face, then heard Joe mumble something. I felt frozen.

I dodged to the right and took off, running back toward the campfire as fast as I could. I didn't stop for a second. I didn't even consider that the sound I'd heard was one of my best friends dying right in front of me, and I couldn't even look into his eyes.

Almost slamming into the tree trunk as the light illuminated more and more, I bolted to the right until I was back in the vast open space, running toward the campfire where the rest of the group was still gathered. My feet pounded the ground hard with each step that I took. My breathing was ragged, and I could feel my body wanting to slow down, but I pushed until I reached the group. Then, I skidded to a stop, bending down and resting my hands on my knees.

The group stared at me wide-eyed as I attempted to catch my breath. I looked at my hands and realized what had splattered across my face.

Blood.

Joe's blood.

The group looked at me horrified, and Mackenzie stepped forward, not saying anything but staring at me. Then, it looked almost as if she was looking through me. Then I noticed Brielle and Jordan looking around me. I turned to find Joe stumbling toward us with the spear that had been in my hands moments earlier, sticking out of his chest. He dropped to his knees like Adam did, falling face-first into the dirt, causing the spear to push back through his body and clatter to the ground.

Another one of my friends was dead, and I was standing there, once again, with blood on my hands.

CHAPTER FIVE
WEDNESDAY, OCTOBER 4TH

Emma is sitting across the room from me, rubbing her temples. I can tell I'm stressing her out and can feel the tension in the room rising. It's almost as if I can read her mind. I know she wants me to complete the questionnaire honestly, but I can't. I'm afraid that if I do, anything that I mark can be misconstrued to lead her to believe that I am the killer. I wasn't the killer that night. I know I wasn't. She will attempt to convince me that our minds will fill in the blanks or that our brains will erase specific memories that are too painful to admit to in our conscious states when someone's personality splits.

I haven't seen this firsthand, but we talked about it in my Psychology class; how Psychologists attempt to explain to people how their splitting personalities work. It's not a one-size-fits-all situation, though. The thought that I could be capable of murder makes me want to break down. I don't want to believe that's the case, but everything feels surreal as I talk about it out loud with Emma. I might be starting to think it was me.

"Jessica," she starts, and my palms immediately begin sweating, "you can't blame me when I say that you could very well be responsible for all of this."

"It wasn't me," I scream at the top of my lungs as I jump off the couch again.

"Jessica, please calm down." Emma is begging now, with tears in her eyes. When did her compassion come back? She was so cold and unfeeling before.

"I'm telling you, it wasn't me," I huff.

"You can't ignore the truth," she says matter of factly, "every death that occurred, you were there. Except the two that were trampled. You were the only one who saw Mark die; you were standing behind Adam when he met his demise, and you were alone with Joe."

She's tapping her pen to the paper pad as she rattles off the notes she's taken.

"How do you explain Bryan and Kaylee?" I challenge.

"You had an accomplice," she accuses.

"I did not have an accomplice." My voice echoes off the walls of the tiny room.

"So you acted alone." Emma thinks she has me cornered now. I'll admit, that was worded very wrong.

"No," I sigh, "I mean, I didn't do it, and I didn't have an accomplice."

I attempt to calm my shaking hands and slow my heart rate by taking a few deep breaths. I scan the room, but there isn't much to look at. I've just now examined my surroundings. I usually kept my head down, walked in, and wandered to the same spot on the couch. We sit in awkward silence for a moment, and I look up at the wall above Emma. I'd never noticed the crucifix hanging just above her desk. It's one of those that you would see at a Catholic church. It is not just a cross, but one that depicts Jesus hanging.

"So, let's say you didn't do it," Emma says, breaking the silence. "Who could have, and why?"

I can't stop staring at the wall decor.

"Jessica?" Emma asks, but I'm stuck inside my own mind. "Jessica."

I snap out of it and look at her. I can feel that my eyes are entirely dead like the lights are on, but no one is home inside my head.

Emma turned to look up at the wall, trying to figure out what I was looking at. Looking at the side of her face, her lips curl upward into a smile, and she turns back to look at me, then back at the crucifix and back to me again.

"Are you religious?" Emma asks me, the question taking me off guard.

"Excuse me?" I reply, confused.

"Are you religious?" She repeats.

"N-not really," my voice shakes as I reply.

"Why not?" She asks, her expression is now filled with concern.

"I don't really buy into all of that."

Emma begins taking more notes. It's not relevant, and I didn't think that religion was supposed to be brought up in these kinds of things. It shouldn't be used as Psychological warfare, which is all that religion is to begin with. I crane my neck as I try to read what she's writing down. I can't see that far, but Emma still covers the notes as though I can.

"That's a shame," she says, her kind eyes boring into me. "As soon as I found religion, my life instantly got better. I felt free. I felt like I had escaped the shackles of what the mainstream world had to offer, and I knew almost immediately that things would be better for the rest of my life. It really could help you, Jess."

Don't talk to me like we are friends.

"I'm good. Religion shackles you more than you know; you're just too blinded by the so-called 'light' to see it," I say. A smirk appears on my face, and I quickly try to hide it.

Emma's eyes are piercing directly into me now, and the color seems to fade from them again. She stands up and walks over to me, sitting beside me on the couch. Her irises are empty black pits as she stares at me. She places an arm over my shoulders, then moves her hand to the top of my back. A cold chill runs down my spine as I feel her touch. I feel so uncomfortable, and then she wraps her fingers around my neck and squeezes. She is still staring into my eyes.

"I'm going to help you, Jess, but I think the way you get past this is to return to where it all happened." Emma's visage takes a turn, and instead of being sweet and caring, I see her expression as dark and threatening.

***

SATURDAY, AUGUST 17TH

I reached my hands up again and swiped more blood off of my face, but it felt like I was just smearing it around. My palms were completely red, and I attempted to wipe them off on the ground, but they were stained at that point, and there was no reason to keep trying. I looked up at the horrified expressions on the faces of those left standing. Mackenzie, Jordan, and Brielle all stared at me, unsure what to do. There was one thing I knew, though. They suspected me without a shred of doubt in their minds.

"I-I-I-" I stammered.

I attempted to force the words past my lips, but they stuck in my throat. My stomach twisted into knots, and I felt like I would be sick. I don't know if it was the thought that they suspected me of murder or the smell of Joe's blood on my face. I swallowed back vomit as it crawled up my throat.

"Jess," Mackenzie whispered, placing her hands over her mouth.

Jordan mainly sat still on the ground, staring at me while sharpening another spear. With increased intensity, he shaved the edges off it, bringing it to an even sharper point than the first one that Joe created. Without a word, I knew what he was thinking: it could all end with one swift stab to the chest.

Tears began streaming down my face as I pled with them not to kill me. I didn't know that was what they were thinking, but I begged as if it were. I fell down to my hands and knees as I screamed like my life depended on it. I'm sure the sheer terror I felt at that moment was palpableI; even the animals among the trees could think re.

Mackenzie walked up and stood above me; I was taller than her, but I felt like she was towering over me at that moment. She stared down at me, her gaze piercing mine, and at that moment, I thought my best friend was going to murder me without a single ounce of remorse. It would have been understandable; the evidence was there that I had killed her boyfriend. Instead of doing the worst, she reached out, offering her hand to pull me off the ground.

"Mack," I whispered quietly through my sobbing with tears and snot running down my face.

"I've got you," she replied, lifting me to my feet.

I couldn't help myself; I threw my arms around Mackenzie and squeezed with every ounce of strength I had left. I heard the breath leave her lungs the harder I embraced. She rested her head on my shoulder as we held on for dear life. I knew she was staring at Joe, but atI didn't care. I had my best friend, and that was all I needed. She eased up and pulled back, staring me in the face and wiping away my tears.

"I-I'm sorry," I said, my eyes pooling up faster than she can clean them off, "I couldn't save him."

"I know," she replied, her eyes filled with tears.

I could see she was trying to keep it together for me, but I could also tell that she wanted to breakdown and cry with me.

"Umm, we're still here," Brielle said suddenly. I'd actually almost forgotten her, but Jordan was still standing there. Her arms crossed over her chest, and an annoyed expression on her face. "And we still think you did it."

Jordan looked at her, surprised. "Speak for yourself," he said. His eyes told an entire story without words. He was sincere and not just trying not to anger the suspected killer.

"I think she's innocent" He gave me a half-smile, but Brielle shot him an angry look.

"I am your girlfriend," she began "You're supposed to be on my side—always."

"That's not how this works," he snapped as he slowly moved closer to Mackenzie and me. "You're being nuts and I won't stand for it."

Brielle snapped a look of surprise and anger in Jordan's direction. You could tell their dynamic by this one single exchange. She was the girlfriend that always had control, even over him, and he'd finally had enough and in that moment, was standing up to her and she didn't appreciate it one bit. He seemed to stand a little taller.

"What did you say to me?" Brielle asked as she bent down.

"You heard me. I won't stand for it. Jessica is innocent." His response echoed through the woods.

Mackenzie and I exchanged a worried glance as Brielle picked up one of the homemade spears and pointed it at Jordan, holding it to his throat.

"You know what I won't stand for?" She asked, pressing it further into his neck. "A disrespectful boyfriend. You've known her for what, a few hours?"

"Brielle, don't do this," I chimed in.

"Shut up, bitch. This doesn't concern you," she threatened.

"If you really think I'm a murderer and you kill Jordan, then you're no better than me." I continued to speak, ignoring her empty threats.

She removed the spear from Jordan's neck and turned it on me. I gulped in anticipation—I was ready for whatever came. She stepped slowly toward me like a killer in a slasher movie. I stood my ground and pushed Mackenzie away to keep her out of the line of fire.

Brielle reached me and placed the sharp end of the spear to my throat, her eyes burning holes into my face. I could see nothing but pure rage in her expression. I gulped again, and the saliva running down my throat pressed into the spear, sending a sharp pain through my neck.

I stood as still as a statue as she pressed harder and harder. I closed my eyes and focused on the pain—it made me feel alive. Just when I thought that the weapon was going to pierce through my flesh, the pain suddenly alleviated. When I opened my eyes, I saw Brielle and Jordan on the ground, rolling around. Jordan was trying to stop her, but it looked like she had a little more strength than he did. It had to be adrenaline running through her system.

"Help me," Jordan yelled.

I immediately jumped into action, grabbing Brielle by the hair to pull her off him. I'm not ab; I'm fighting dirty and willing to do whatever it took. She turned her attention back to me again as she jumped to her feet. She threw punch after punch, striking me in the abdomen a couple of times. Jordan got back up and jumped on her back. I'll admit, I'll really be more robust than she looked.

She lost her balance as Jordan shifted her weight just right and fell over, knocking him back to the ground. I grabbed her and lifted her up, landing a few blows to the side of her face.

"Mack, help," I screamed. When I looked back, Mackenzie looked horrified, frozen in place. She wasn't a fighter. I knew with that expression that I was on my own.

I grabbed Brielle by the shirt and extended my arms, keeping as much distance between us as possible. Then, I pulled her close to me and flipped her around, trying to disorient her. No matter how much she struggled to get away, I kept a firm grip on her shirt. I wasn't going to let her get away.

Her back was to the fire, and she yelped in pain as I backed her closer to it. I looked back at Jordan, and he nodded. I cocked back and landed another blow to the side of her face. Blood spewed from her mouth, and she spit it in my face.

I pulled her close one more time, pressing my nose to hers.

"You still think I'm a killer?" The rhetorical question came out menacing. It even shocked me as the words came from my mouth.

"Yes," she replied with a smirk on her face. She spit more blood at me.

"Good. Because now I am."

Her eyes widened and I pushed her back with all the force I had left in me. She stumbled back, falling into the bonfire pit. For a moment, I felt regret for the action, but she had it coming. I turned back and looked at Jordan. He was forcing back a devious smile, but I could see it tugging at the corners of his mouth.

I turned back and watched Brielle struggle to scramble back to her feet and pull herself from the fire. She hopped up, and her clothes were ablaze. There was nothing any of us could do. The screaming that she let out was terrifying. Burning to death has to be one of the worst ways to go.

She dropped to the ground and attempted to snuff out the flames, but there was no point. I watched as she rolled around, leaving burning pieces of flesh behind. It only took a couple of minutes before she stopped moving. The three of us left behind stood still as statues.

After a couple of minutes, the fire died down, and I felt the presence of two bodies next to me. I looked over to find Jordan on my left and Mackenzie on my right. I turned and stared at Jordan, unsure what to say. I opened my mouth to speak, but he held up a hand.

"Not necessary," he said, "she was a nightmare." I know he didn't mean that, because he reached up and wiped a tear away from his cheek that he was trying to hold in and his lips were trembling.

In my attempt to prove that I wasn't a sadistic killer, I became one.

"And then there were three," Jordan said.

We stood silent as we peered into the woods, anticipating what might happen next.

CHAPTER SIX
WEDNESDAY, OCTOBER 4TH

"So you remember one of the murders," Emma says, still implying that I was responsible for all of them.

"I remember all of the murders," I start, returning the same condescending tone she gave me, "because I witnessed all of them."

"You mean that you committed them," she snaps back.

"I did not," I scream at the top of my lungs again, and return to my feet, staring down at Emma, making myself feel bigger than her.

The room feels like it's closing in on me. I can feel my heart beginning to speed up, and my breathing is becoming erratic. I think I'm having a panic attack. The room starts spinning, and my limbs feel like they no longer exist. My eyes dart around the room, looking for anything I can to ground myself.

It's not the first time I've had one, but the worse it seems to become each time it happens. Every time a panic attack comes on, it's like I forget everything I've been taught in the last couple of months about fending them off. I have to focus on my thoughts and try to remember the steps to fight them.

I sit back down, but this time, it is Emma's chair across the room. I need to get away from her. I can't be here anymore; forget what I said earlier, I need out. I refuse to give her any more of my time. She stands up and approaches me, her hands outstretched toward me. I throw my arms up in front of my face as if shielding myself from a fire.

I jump up and head for the door, lunging at the handle but missing it by just an inch or two. I fall to the ground, and my face slams into the hard ground. I look down and see blood dripping from my nose and reach up, one last time. Checking behind me, Emma continues to skulk toward me; I've never seen her in this light before. Just her presence makes the room feel like it goes cold.

My hand is stretched out for the door handle, but I can't quite reach it. My legs feel entirely numb.

It's all in your head, I think to myself; *your legs aren't actually paralyzed.*

But all I can do is stretch for the door and hope to extend my fingers enough to grab onto it. That's precisely what I do after what feels like an eternity. I can feel the cold metal as it touches my palm, and I grip tight, attempting to turn it, but it doesn't budge.

Did Emma lock the door? Why would she—

The question inside my head trails off as I feel her presence coming closer to me. I don't dare to look. I don't want to know what she might do to me. I shut my eyes tightly as I recognize her touch on my back.

"Jessica," she says, her voice sounding callous and unfeeling. It doesn't make me feel calm as it usually does. A chill runs down my spine as I hear my name slip past her lips.

"No." It's all I can muster. One simple word.

"Jessica, it's okay," she says. Her voice has an underlying gritty tone.

Her hands press harder into the small of my back. I can feel my vertebrae popping as she applies more pressure. Then she lets go and reaches for my hand; I tuck it underneath my body between myself and the floor in an attempt to keep it from her. I feel so weak; I can't hold it. She grabs it and folds my arm up like a pretzel behind me. Then grabs the other and does the same.

I hear a zipping sound, and then a sudden pain in my wrists, and I can feel a slight pulling on my shoulders. I really can't move now. She's handcuffed me. The plastic material that I can feel against my skin tells me she used zip ties to restrain me.

Then, I feel a tugging at the waist of my blue jeans, and a sudden cold chill runs up my spine as my skin is exposed to the air in the room. Another sharp pain shoots through my body, and I feel suddenly relaxed; the tenseness in my muscles is slowly melting away, and my eyelids are quickly becoming heavier.

"What," I squeak out, "what did you do?"

"Shh," Emma says, "it'll all be okay. I promise."

"Wh-why," I whisper.

A single tear falls from my eyes and rolls down my cheek. It splashes to the floor.

My head is spinning now, and I can't open my eyelids. I feel relaxed but too comfortable. It feels like the medicine they give you before surgery to calm you down is coursing through my veins.

I can't keep my eyes open now, and every sound in the room is becoming muffled until there is nothing more to hear, and my world turns to black.

***

SATURDAY, AUGUST 17TH

We stared into the woods for a while. I'm unsure how long it had been, but it was a while. The three of us didn't speak, not a single syllable. I don't think any of us even moved a single muscle. It was evident then that none of us had a plan, not even an inkling of what we should do.

It seemed we were at odds with whoever was doing this to us, and I know an even bigger question than "who": "why?" It seemed completely random to attack a music festival the way they did. I'm guessing the psychopath figured it was the best way to kill as many as possible without getting caught with all of the commotion going on.

Anger was bubbling in the pit of my stomach; mad that our night was ruined, furious that we didn't know why they were doing this to us, and downright pissed—not even sad at that point—that two of my friends were dead. I made a promise to myself at that moment that I wouldn't go down like they did; I would fight until the very end, even if that meant taking a bullet to the head.

The smoke around Brielle's body had thinned out and was only periodically wafting into the air around her. Finally, I turned around and walked away from the fire pit, realizing that the side of my face was on fire. Jordan and Mackenzie followed suit, but still, none of us spoke a word. I don't think we knew what to say even if we had. I didn't know what I could say to make Jordan feel better. I had, after all, just killed his girlfriend.

As the three of us aimlessly wandered around to figure out our next move, I moved closer to Jordan and threw an arm over his shoulders.

"Jordan," I started, but he attempted to look away.

This same man had just told me that Brielle was a nightmare and didn't seem to feel bad about what had transpired at all.

"Jordan," I said again, more forcefully, while placing my hands on his cheeks, forcing him to look at me.

He didn't look at me, but through me. It was as if I wasn't even there, but I chose to ignore it.

"I know saying sorry doesn't do jack shit right now," I began. My eyes started to well up with tears, "but I want you to know that I am sorry. I'm sorry for doing that to Brielle, I'm sorry about Bryan and Kaylee, I'm sorry about this whole damn night."

Finally, he looked at me as if I existed again. His beautiful green eyes were a welcome change to the darkness that surrounded us. I looked deeply into them, and he looked even deeper back into mine. It was almost as if he had found his person within me. I was reading too deeply into it.

"I'm not mad," he said, "sure, I'm sad, but I'm not mad at you, and knowing Brielle, had you not done it, she definitely would have thrown you into that fire. Then we'd really be screwed out here."

"What do you mean?" I asked, genuinely confused.

"You've proven yourself to be the most capable in this situation. Without you, we wouldn't have even made it this far."

I giggled. There's no way he meant that.

"Yeah, because I've been so helpful up to this point," I said, full of self-doubt.

"You've at least tried." His entire being was calming; I felt so grounded being near him. "I don't think we'd have made it this far without you, and I thank you for that."

"We haven't made it anywhere. Look around you; there are dead bodies everywhere." My reply sounded cold, even for me.

"Well, yeah, there is that."

"Just know I'm so sorry about Brielle; we will leave it as is."

I released my grip on his face and turned to talk to Mackenzie, sitting about twenty feet away from us.

"One more thing," Jordan said.

"Yeah?" I asked.

"Don't let me die too." He smiled.

"I'll do my best."

I turned again and started walking toward Mackenzie. She was sitting in a fetal position. Her knees were to her chest, and her arms wrapped around them. The only thing missing was her rocking back and forth in a padded room, and I'd have thought she'd completely lost it.

"Mack?" I approached her softly. I was afraid of what the evening had done to her mental state.

She turned to look at me, and I noticed for the first time that night that she had dark circles around her eyes—she looked exhausted. We all were at that point in the evening, but we needed to continue pressing on. She reached up and wiped her face with her arm, and I realized it wasn't exhaustion weighing on her; it was everything else going on.

I continued to press on and didn't let anything weigh me down, so I didn't realize the effect everything had on everyone else. I knew how Jordan was feeling, but shook the reminder out of my mind that I had become a murderer in an effort to defeat one.

"Yeah," Mackenzie sniffled.

"You doing okay, babe?" I asked, even though I knew the answer. I kneeled down next to her and placed a hand on her shoulder.

She looked at me like it was the dumbest question she'd ever been asked, but what else do you say to someone in the situation we had found ourselves in? I didn't know, so I said the first thing that came to mind. She put her head down again, resting it on her hands. I patted her shoulder and stood back up. There was nothing I could do to comfort her.

I turned toward Jordan, and he shook his head in disbelief. It felt so surreal that we were even dealing with what we were, and all three of us wanted to give up. Just sit and wait for death to come; it was what I was thinking, but I didn't want to say that out loud. I had unintentionally made myself the leader of our survival. It seemed everyone was leaning on me to find a way to make it through the night, and I wasn't sure why.

Suddenly, Jordan's eyes widened, and he lifted a hand, pointing toward Mackenzie.

"M-M-Mackenzie," he stuttered.

I turned around quickly and looked over as she looked up at the two of us. All I could do was stare at her wide-eyed as I was face to-face with the killer, standing over her with a hatchet. It was the closest we had been all night, and I felt like it was our opportunity to take them down.

Jordan must have considered the same as he bent down and picked up the last spear that had been sharpened. It seemed that he was ready for a fight.

Mackenzie turned her head to look at us and opened her mouth to speak, but she didn't have enough time to get the words out.

The killer swung quickly, burying the hatchet into Mackenzie's back, and she let out a howl as it ripped through her flesh. Blood immediately began spewing from her mouth, and I knew then that I was about to watch my best friend die. The killer pulled it out of her and swiftly swung again, creating another crater in her body.

At that moment, Jordan and I jumped into action, running toward the killer with everything we had. I wasn't sure what I was supposed to do as I didn't have a weapon. Still, I figured that if I could subdue them by jumping on their back, Jordan might have an opportunity to stab at the person with the spear.

The killer ripped the hatchet from Mackenzie's body one last time, and she fell to the ground with a sickening thud. Instead of stopping to help her, we ran as the person took off into the woods. We pushed through the dark brush as fast as we could, following the sound of their footsteps on the dried leaves and other brush they were running up against. I held my arms out in front of myself to stop rogue branches from smacking me in the face.

The deeper we went, the darker the woods seemed. It was disorienting, and the forest seemed to continue on forever. It felt like we were running in circles, and suddenly, the only footsteps I could hear were my own and Jordan's as he stayed by my side.

"Jordan," I yelled.

"What?" He shouted back.

"Stop."

The two of us skidded to a halt, and the only thing I could hear was the sound of us panting as we attempted to catch our breath. Eventually, that quieted, and the forest was completely silent. A couple of owls hooted overhead, but other than that, nothing.

I turned around, and I could no longer see any illumination from our bonfire. The person led us deep into the woods, and we didn't have any clue how to get back. We shouldn't have chased them. We should have let them run, but both of our fight-or-flight responses went into overdrive, and we weren't thinking clearly.

I reached my hand out and touched the fabric of Jordan's shirt. I felt as his hand brushed against mine and then gripped me. I knew I was safe for the most part, but I could only think of one thing.

My best friend was dying.
Cold.
Alone.
Scared.

CHAPTER SEVEN
WEDNESDAY, OCTOBER 4TH

It's dark and cramped in here. I can't tell where I am. No matter how often I blink, all I see is black; I'm not even sure my eyes are opening. I feel around, and the palms of my hands rub on some rough fabric all around me. It feels like I'm inside of a coffin. My heart is racing as I come to, and my breathing is erratic.

Calm down, Jess.

I pat the ground underneath myself, and still, all I can feel is the same fabric that covers the walls and the roof. Finally, I touch something cold and made of metal. It curves at the end, and it almost feels like a crowbar. I touch the tip of it, and I can feel the rounded edge; it resembles the shape of a nut that someone would thread onto a bolt. Tire iron.

SNAP.

SNAP.

SNAP.

The makeshift bracelet on my wrist brings me comfort as I snap it as hard as I can on my arm.

Suddenly, a loud banging sound, followed by a crashing feeling, jostles me around, and I think I know where I am now. I'm specifically in the back of Emma's car, the trunk. We had hit a pothole, and it didn't feel too good as my head bounced up and down on the rigid platform.

I'm digging deep into my memories, but I can't remember much past talking to her on the couch only a little while ago. I can't dig up what led me here or why she would do this to me. I came to her for help. I trusted her. I trusted all of them, but every single one failed me.

I remember that all trunks had a safety release hanging from the lid, and I began searching above me for something to pull on, but I couldn't find it.

BANG.

Another pothole.

It feels like Emma is driving like a crazy person. I think the car shifts to the right or left every few seconds as if she's trying to flee from the cops. I hear horns honking around the car as we drive down the road, merging from lane to lane.

Reaching into my pocket, I feel nothing. My phone is gone—I have no way to call for help. Panic begins setting in more potent, and I try my best to breathe slowly. In the trunk of her car, I have limited oxygen. If I use it all up, I could fall into a deep sleep again but never come out of it. Maybe that's Emma's plan—to kill me.

But why?

I ball my hands into fists and start banging on the trunk lid as hard as I can, trying to signal to other drivers that I need help. Maybe we will drive past a pedestrian, and they will hear me. The car slams to a stop.

"Quiet down back there." Emma's voice is entirely emotionless as the words come from her mouth. It's like nothing I've ever heard before, especially from her. It's not the usual, comforting voice I've learned from my therapist.

The vehicle seems older, based on the material I can feel lining the trunk. I remember hearing somewhere that the backseats should pop open with enough force. They aren't like the new ones with latches and a physical switch that needs to be activated. I turn my body and place my feet flat on the backs of the second-row seats. I cock my knees back and slam my feet down onto the surface.

It doesn't move.

I try it repeatedly until I feel the seats start giving way. The only problem now is that if I'm able to get these to open and crawl through, I don't have any other plan in place. What am I going to do once I get out of here? I'll have to think on my feet.

"Don't you dare, Jessica," Emma growls.

I slam my feet on the seatbacks again, and it flips forward. I scramble and crawl through, landing myself on the seat. Emma looks at me in the rearview. The darker color of her eyes has returned, but I can only see it when we pass a street light. She pulls the steering wheel a hard left, and we start driving down a dirt two-track road. There is nothing around us but trees.

I look down onto the vehicle's floor, and a couple of large zip ties lie on the floor. For a moment, I look at my wrists and realize my skin is burning. I remember Emma zip-tying my hands together with makeshift handcuffs.

Why did she remove them?

I grab the tie from the floor and do everything I can think of. I throw it around Emma's neck and grab it from the other side of her head. I pull back as hard as I can, and she jerks the wheel all over the road, trying to get me off of her. She keeps moving forward, and I firmly grip the ties. She starts gagging and choking on the pressure against her throat, but I don't let up.

I glance out the window and notice the trees around us are becoming thinner until the woods open up into a clearing. Emma notices, too, and slams on the brakes. I fly forward and knock my face against the back of the headrest so hard that I begin to see stars in my field of vision. I shake my head to try to clear my disorientation, and I look around us. Emma exits the car and opens my door, grabbing me by the legs.

She pulls me out, and I land on the cold, hard ground. Emma stands above me, and I look back at her with terrified eyes. I attempt to jump to my feet, but she slams the heel of her pumps down into my stomach. Squirming and writhing in pain, my tear-filled eyes skew my vision, and I can barely see her. Suddenly, Emma grabs me by my shirt, lifting me to my feet.

Emma backs away from me about fifteen feet and stares back. She doesn't say a word; the crazed look on her face makes me think she's finally cracked. Years of listening to everyone else describe their problems, having freakouts in her office, and having to be institutionalized under her care have finally made her snap.

SNAP.

My mind tells me that snapping the rubber band will make me feel better, even now, so I try to ignore it.

The pain in my stomach is spreading to my back, and I have to choke back the pain. I want to scream, but Emma has brought me to a remote area with no one around.

What is she going to do to me?

I look around some more, and I look down to my feet. Where I'm standing is a patch of black etched into the dirt. I notice a single, charred piece of wood next to my right foot. I looked up, and the expression on my face must have told Emma that I realized where I was. She has a maniacal look on her face, and suddenly, she pulls out a knife and points it at me.

Emma has brought me back to the festival grounds.

***

SATURDAY, AUGUST 17TH

"What are we going to do?" I asked Jordan hastily. I spun in circles, trying to find any semblance of the fire illuminating the area, but I couldn't see anything.

We were completely lost.

"I don't know." His voice sounded calm, but I could detect a slight shake in his words.

I pulled out my phone and turned on the flashlight. I noticed the screen was suddenly cracked, but I didn't know what happened to cause it. Jordan followed suit and pulled him out, flicking on his flashlight. They didn't provide too much light, but it was better than nothing.

"I think we came from that direction," Jordan said, pointing.

"Maybe we should just start walking. It's not like we can get any more lost." I replied.

"You sure about that?" The light from our phones shone enough that I could see a smirk on his face.

"Nope."

I began walking anyway, trudging through mud and other debris littering the forest floor. The further we walked, the darker it seemed to become, but I assumed it was just my eyes playing tricks on me. Every now and then, we could hear rustling nearby, but when no one made themselves known, we chalked it up to be an animal.

We walked in nearly complete silence, and I wasn't sure if both of us were trying to remain quiet so we could hear what was going on around us or if Jordan was harboring significant resentment toward me for what I did to Brielle. I was sure it was a bit of both, but I was torn on whether I wanted the answer. He told me everything was okay, but I'm sure it wasn't. I tried putting myself in his shoes, imagining what it would feel like if some random person I didn't know had killed my significant other—that made me feel worse. I needed to say something, or I would stew on it, and we had much bigger problems.

"Jordan," I said, "I don't know—I mean—if we both make it out of this, I don't know how I will ever make up for what I did to you."

"You don't have to do anything." His voice was soft and reassuring.

"Yes, I do," I replied.

"No, you don't. I know you don't know us well, but Brielle was," he paused, and I waited on bated breath, "different. She was erratic; I never knew what she would do next. I could have never anticipated that she would attack you. You did what you needed to do to save yourself, and I fully understand self-defense."

"Yeah, but," I started.

"But nothing," Jordan replied with a genuine smile.

I sighed and continued pressing on through the wilderness, hoping for a miracle to lead us back to the bonfire. Prayer wasn't my thing, but I begged and pleaded for the universe to return us. Walking through the woods was just asking to be attacked without knowing what was coming.

Just then, a faint orange glow appeared in the distance as if the planets aligned perfectly. It was five hundred feet in front of us. I couldn't believe what I was seeing and began thinking that maybe wishful thinking was causing me to hallucinate. Then, Jordan stopped dead in his tracks when he noticed it. The two of us stared at the rumbling fire for a couple of seconds, and then Jordan took off running as fast as he could. It took me a moment to realize this, and I pushed forward as fast as possible.

We just about jumped through the tree line as the fire fully came into our view, and we had to skid to a halt as we hit the dirt of the festival grounds. I never thought I would be happy to be back there, but it beat being stuck in the woods all night. It took a bit, but we caught our breath, and I sat down in front of the fire, staring into it, reliving the moment that Brielle fell into the flames. It played on repeat in my head.

Jordan came over and sat down beside me, imitating my actions and staring into the fire for a moment.

"You know," he said, "if we are going to be stuck out here all night, we should probably check around in the tents for food. I'm getting kind of hungry."

I hadn't noticed until he mentioned it, but my stomach was rumbling, too. I stood up immediately and held my hand out to him, offering to help him up.

"You're right," I agreed.

He took my hand, and I pulled him back to his feet. We walked immediately over to the tents and began ransacking them, looking for anything we could to shove into our mouths. I didn't find much, a couple of bags of chips and some packages of cookies, but other than that, there wasn't much to keep us full until morning.

I pulled out my phone and checked the time, realizing it was 3:37 AM. The sun would start rising over the trees in just a few hours. That's all we had to make. It was only a bit longer. If anything, we would survive, and I'd have a new friend. It would probably be a long, uphill battle with the law, but I knew I would have someone who could corroborate my story. At the worst, we'd both be dead, and none of this would be our problem.

I started shoving the snacks I found into my pockets and could hear Jordan moving about in the tent next to me. Suddenly, his movements sounded more sudden and rougher. I popped out of the tent and observed the one he was in. It rattled around, and the canvas on the top was wiggling like crazy. I walked up to it.

"Jordan?" I asked but heard no reply. The tent just kept shaking like a leaf.

"Jordan." I was screaming his name.

Suddenly, the tent stopped shaking, and everything went still. There wasn't even a sound coming from inside the tent. Then, the zipper began sliding around the front door of the tent. I backed away. My heart was pounding, and my hands began to shake. My legs were quaking, and I did everything in my power to keep myself upright and not fall to the ground.

A dark figure appeared directly before me; only ten feet of empty space stood between us. They were wearing all black—a long robe that reminded me of Ghostface and a hood covering their face. I glanced behind the person brooding in front of me. I saw Jordan's lifeless body lying face down on the ground of the tent, covered in blood, his eyes still wide open.

I stared at them, and they stared back at me, or so I thought, but I couldn't see their eyes.

"And then, there was one," a female's voice said menacingly as she slid a knife out of her sleeve.

CHAPTER EIGHT
WEDNESDAY, OCTOBER 4TH

Emma is still holding the knife out toward me, threateningly, but doesn't say a word. She stares at me, and the smile on her face is spreading from ear to ear. It's unsettling, to say the least. I look around but am careful not to take my eyes off her for too long. She could act quickly, and I need to be ready; she's armed, and I'm not. I'm not sure what I will do if she comes to me.

"Emma, you did this?" I ask, my voice is trembling.

Silence. She stares at me with a crazed look in her eyes.

"Emma, answer me," I growl.

"Yes. I did it." Her voice is low and calm, as in most of our sessions.

"Why?" My eyes are filling with tears as she confesses to the murders.

Emma flips the knife and holds it with her whole palm, her fingers wrapped tightly around the handle. It looks like she's about to cock back and swing down as hard as she can. Instead, she begins to pace in front of me.

"Why is it," she starts, "that when someone is faced with a killer, their first question is 'why?' It's exactly like a horror movie; it's pathetic. Why does there ever need to be a motive? Why can't anyone just kill for the simple reason that they want to?"

"Even now, you're being a therapist. Why do you need to answer a question with a question?"

She roars with laughter, which echoes through the trees. In the distance, I hear a flock of birds flapping their wings hard as they fly away.

"You want a motive, Jessica? Is that really what you want?" She asks.

I don't say anything, just nod my head.

"God. The lord. The almighty father. Yahweh. Do you get it?"

Perplexed, I stare at her, "No, I don't."

"Satan. Lucifer. Baphomet. The devil," she growls.

"One of these things is not like the other," I retort.

Frustrated, Emma stomps her feet like a spoiled child that isn't getting their way. She runs toward me but stops mid-way, trying to intimidate me. I back up a few feet to keep the distance between us.

"The lord above has chosen me to silence those who perpetrate evil. Heavy metal is the devil's music, and I will not tolerate those who participate in a ritual of evil. God wants me to rid the Earth of the wickedness that poisons our youth and to help him lead more young people to the holy land," Emma said suddenly.

Emma's expression is one of seriousness, but I can't help but let out a chuckle. Her face changes immediately to anger in response. I hand over my mouth to stifle the laughter, but it does no good. I continue to howl in anticipation of what's next.

"Do you think that cleansing this world is funny?" She growls, "This is serious. Our world is in trouble, and if everyone is not saved, everyone will burn in a pit of fire and brimstone. Do you want that for eternity for yourself?"

"Wait, wait, wait," I say, still laughing, "so hold on, let me get this straight. You came to a metal music festival because you think the music is satanic, and, in the name of God, you murdered people to save them. I don't know the teachings of Jesus very well, but I'm pretty sure that one of the first rules for life on earth is 'thou shalt not kill.'"

Really, what's transpiring is no laughing matter; people died. Families faced the harsh reality that their loved ones would not return home. That included some of my best friends, and I had to be the one to break the news to them. I can't believe that I am actually hearing what I'm hearing.

"If the lord calls upon you to do his bidding, then you must answer the call, or else you answer to Saint Peter at the pearly gates, and he will send you straight to hell. I, for one, am not interested in burning for all of eternity when I die," Emma states. "But now, God above has allowed me to finish the job he has tasked me with."

"How so?" I ask, but I know exactly what she's saying.

"I prayed and prayed for an answer. I begged God to show me that my job was done and that I had completed what he asked me."

"And I'm sure he came down, sitting on a cloud, telling you exactly what he needed from you," I giggle.

"That's not how faith works, Jessica. He showed me that I hadn't completed my job. He showed me by sending you my way. My colleagues and I talk; we talk about clients. As soon as your previous therapist showed me that he wasn't up to snuff to do the job, to make you better, and shared your story with me, I requested you. God works in mysterious ways, and the sooner you learn, the better off you'll be. You better come to terms with it quick because you're going to be dead soon. I won't let you live because God wants me to kill you—to rid this world of your evil-doing."

I begin to pace, matching the eerie tone Emma is trying to set. I stand a little taller and show her I'm not one to be messed with. I can't back down now. Not now that I'm so close to ending this once and for all. Unlike her, I will end her life and not bat an eye, I don't have the fear in me of a deity like she does, and I have something to fight for. Revenge runs deep for Mackenzie, Adam, and Joe, for Jordan and everyone else who died that night. I know that deep down, she is harboring a lot of remorse for what she did, but religion is blinding her from seeing the truth in her actions.

"You don't get to kill me yet," I warn, "because I need to know more. Don't take me from this world without giving me the satisfaction of truly knowing why."

"I've already told you why," Emma says. She sounds annoyed.

"Answer this: why me? Why my friends? Why that night of all nights?" I ask.

"You think I chose you and your friends? I didn't. I chose that festival, and that was it. All of you frolicking, enjoying yourselves while committing sin, suckling from the teat of Baphomet. Listening and dancing to that sickening music that brings glory and power to the kingdom of Satan. I didn't know you from Adam, but I chose that festival because I knew it was my best chance to rid this world of as much evil as possible in one evening." Emma's confession sounds insane.

"You and your whole generation, all in attendance, disgusted me. I did the world a favor by removing as many of you as I did from this plane of existence. And it was all for moral reasons as opposed to the immorality that was displayed that night. Simply put, you and your friends were in danger only because you were there."

"Don't you dare talk about my friends," I threaten, "you don't know shit about them, or me, or anyone else that was there. You're so blinded by this so-called 'light' that your God brings that you will stop at nothing to force it down the throats of anyone who will listen. You should look into a mirror sometime; you and your whole world disgust me. It's sick, and everything you do in the name of religion—doesn't make you better than anyone. It makes you a hypocrite."

Emma begins sauntering toward me. She's twirling the knife between the palm of her hand and the sharp end carefully balanced on her index finger. The crazy smile has appeared on her face again, and I back up, still keeping distance between us. As I do, I trip and fall backward on a rock, scrambling backward as I try to keep her away from me. She takes the opportunity and runs toward me, lunging forward and landing on my body.

She's smiling directly into my eyes as she takes the knife handle in both hands and raises it above me.

This is it.

Emma begins laughing; it's high-pitched and hurts my ears as it rings through the air. It's almost as if she's possessed by an actual demon.

Her thighs don't have a natural grip on my body. If I focus all of my energy and strength on my lower body, I might be able to get her off of me.

"Father, forgive me," she announces.

She swings the knife downward, directly at my face, and her hips lift just enough off of me. I jerk my body to the right, and she goes flying off of me. I scramble back to my feet and assume a fighting position.

"You could make this easy, Jessica," she says as she wipes the dirt off her dress, "let me save you."

"I'd rather burn in hell than spend eternity in heaven with you if you actually make it there," I announce, "I'm not going down without a fight. Not this time."

Emma lifts her hands and tilts her head backward in a praying stance. Her lips are moving rapidly, and I begin to think she's actually praying. This is my opportunity. I charge her like a raging bull and throw my arms out. As I plunge into her body, I wrap my hands around her, and the surprise tosses the knife out of her hands as she crashes to the ground.

"Just you and me," I said cockily. A smile pulls at the corners of my mouth, "now it's a fair fight."

"You don't want to—"Emma starts.

I swing with all my might, and Emma's jaw cracks under the force of my fist hitting her face. Another swing from the other side.

I continue this system until I can feel my knuckles getting wet from blood spewing out of her mouth. Her arm stretches outward, and she makes an attempt to grab the knife, but it's too far away.

I reach for her arm anyway and pull it back to her body. I'm not taking any chances.

"Give up, you're not going to win this," I warn.

"I've got God on my side," she replies.

Out of the corner of my eye, the moonlight shines and reflects off the knife's blade. It's as if the universe is showing me the answer to everything. The universe is telling me to grab the knife. I want to plunge it into her heart and listen to her beg for her life. I want to watch the light leave her eyes as she forced me to endure with every single one of my friends that night during the festival.

Do I take a chance and jump off of Emma and rush to the blade, or do I stay here, keeping her secured?

The light glimmering off the blade catches my eye, and I take it as a sign. I land another punch to the side of her face in an attempt to disorient her and scramble to my feet, running for the knife. I grab it and turn around, holding it out threateningly in Emma's direction.

We face off momentarily, and I watch her shoulders rise and fall; she's trying to catch her breath. Her wide, blood-covered smile shows as she grits her teeth at me. She's going to make an attempt at getting the knife back from me.

Suddenly, I feel like I'm being stared at from behind. It's an unsettling feeling that sends shivers down my spine. I turn my head slowly, being careful not to take my eyes off Emma for too long.

From my peripheral, I see a figure skulking up from behind, but I can't see their face. I turn so that I can keep both of them in my sights and back up, waving the knife in both directions.

Fight or flight is taking over, and I'm planted to the ground. Apparently, my mind is choosing to fight, though I'm unsure of how I will fight my way out of this. Two against one. Finally, the second figure steps closer, and I can see their face. Male, about six foot tall, with perfectly manicured hair. My eyes widen.

"Jordan?" I ask, stunned.

CHAPTER NINE
SATURDAY, AUGUST 17TH

The two of us stood motionless for a moment; I was staring at her, and I think she was staring at me. The hood around her face minimized what I could see of her expression. She held the knife out at me, mimicking stabbing motions in my direction. Even though sheer terror was coursing through my entire being, I kept my visage stoic to show her no fear. People like that feed on the fear they can hear in your voice or sense in your movements. I refused to let her know she had gotten me through like that.

I looked behind her one last time, glancing at Jordan, and a pang of sadness ran through my body, sending chills up my spine. I'd watched my own friends, along with several others that I didn't know, die that night, but for some reason, Jordan's death had felt different. The two of us had formed a connection in the brief time we had together, and I had thought he'd have been a good ally. Someone who was here, with me, experienced everything I could lean on if needed and vice versa.

Suddenly, anger radiated through my entire being like a roaring fire, like the fire smoldering away behind me. It was like nothing I'd ever felt before, and I felt like I could take on any threat that came my way. Something told me I would survive this, but I wasn't sure how. I just knew that I had to fight like hell.

"This ends with me," I warned.

"You're right," the masked woman said, her tone telling me she had a smile spreading across her face. It does end with you. Dead."

"Not a chance, bitch." I knew that I was doing nothing more than antagonizing her, but there wasn't much else I could do. I wasn't even sure how I was going to defend myself. At that point, I needed to use whatever means necessary to ensure survival. I needed to get that knife.

Before she could speak, I turned around and ran toward the bonfire. It was the only thing that I could think to do. I skidded to a stop and reached down, grabbing the largest burning branch I could find. I thought if I could touch her long, flowing robe with it, I could light her on fire. It was the only thing I could consider, but I knew I had to keep coming up with new plans, just in case that didn't work.

I glanced back and saw her chasing after me as I held out the makeshift torch in her direction. She realized what I was thinking because she came to a screeching halt, keeping the distance between us. It was like a movie; we rotated in a circle, keeping our eyes trained on one another. She kept the knife held out in my direction, and I did the same with the tree limb.

Out of nowhere, I saw her head turn and look toward the woods. She darted into the tree line, and I took off behind her. I attempted to keep her in my sights, but she was quickly swallowed by the forest's darkness. I stopped and listened as carefully as possible, listening for any cue that she was moving. Some rustling among the trees could be heard, but when Jordan and I were walking earlier, I couldn't tell if it was the killer or an animal. The burning branch wasn't offering much light to help me.

I stared into the woods, scanning side to side, attempting to adjust my eyesight to the dark, hoping to catch something. Just then, a voice rang out from behind me.

"You can't stop me." I turned, and she was standing a few feet away. I did a double take, looking between her and the woods, confused as to how she got around me as quickly as she did. "I know these woods. I know how to move around undetected. I'd studied them before this metal music festival began." The way she stressed the word metal made it sound like she was disgusted by the genre as a whole.

"I can and I will," I shouted confidently, "I don't care how well you know your way around. All I need is one thing."

The killer roared with laughter as my voice echoed through the woods and took a step toward me. Then another.

Come on, just a little closer.

"And what's that?" She laughed, taking yet another step in my direction.

I raised my eyebrows at her arrogantly, pulled back, and sliced through the air with the burning tree limb in my hand, stabbing her in the gut. It didn't set her on fire as anticipated, but it did much more in my favor. She stumbled backward but couldn't catch her balance. As she fell to the ground, the knife went soaring through the air, and I couldn't waste even one second. I tossed the branch to the side and ran toward the knife as her back crashed to the dirt floor. As I reached it, I did a baseball slide and grabbed onto it.

I stood back up, pointing the knife at her. She held her hands up, and I couldn't tell if she was being serious or doing it mockingly. My hand holding the blade began to shake as adrenaline shot through every fiber of my being, and I couldn't calm it. Even though I knew it wouldn't help, I grabbed onto the handle with my other hand to steady myself. Then, I realized she was messing with me as her laughter bounced through the forest again.

"I don't need that to kill you." As the words left her lips, she ran into the woods again.

I twirled around in circles, ensuring I kept my eyes peeled on my surroundings. It felt like the trees were closing in on me, and all the sounds coming from the deepest parts of the woods disoriented me to the point where I couldn't pinpoint anything specific. Every twig snapping and rustling made me jump out of my skin—even the crackling of the fire still smoldering next to me made me twitch.

I was being watched from every angle and wished Jordan was still with me. Inside my head, it felt like all was lost, and I knew I was going to die; I couldn't let her know that, though. Fighting through it was the only way I could give myself any chance at survival, but I could feel myself weakening by the minute. I was tired, and I wasn't sure how much longer I would last.

A crunching sound rang out behind me, and I turned quickly. Faster than I had reacted to the sound, I was slammed in the head with something heavy. Blinding pain shot through my entire body, and before I knew it, I was lying on the ground looking at the stars, the edge of my vision becoming blurry. As I blinked through it, attempting to see more clearly, a figure stepped over me, and I could see what I was hit with; a large rock.

At first, I thought it was her coming to finish me off, but the person knelt down next to me, their face hanging over mine. They placed a finger over what I'd assumed was their lips, telling me to be quiet—they also had a hood covering their face. They leaned in closer, and I could feel their hot breath in my ear. Tears welled in my eyes as I assumed that would be the end. I stared at the stars through even more blurred vision, taking in everything before I was gone forever.

"I need you to calm yourself; calm your breathing, slow your heart rate, and stay still." A familiar man's voice spoke slowly into my ear.

"If you want to live, you will do as you're told. Do you understand?"

I nodded at him in understanding. Even though the voice was familiar, I couldn't pinpoint it. I couldn't figure it out, but for some reason, I trusted him. Something in my heart told me to trust him with everything I had. I closed my eyes slowly as I faded out. I wasn't sure if I was dying or if I was going unconscious; all I knew was that I was slipping into some sort of sleep.

"I've got you." Those were the last words I'd heard before the world fell into darkness. That was my last memory of the festival.

CHAPTER TEN
WEDNESDAY, OCTOBER 4TH

"Grab her, Jordan," Emma snarls.

Jordan runs up to me with a ferocity that glues my feet to the ground. I can't move, and part of me doesn't want to run away from the man I got to know over a single night. His gritted teeth and wicked smile make my body go rigid, and before I know it, he's behind me. He grabs my arms and folds them behind my back; the pressure on my shoulders causes me to wince.

Emma turns around and walks back to the car, where she begins rummaging around in the backseat. Jordan leans in, and his hot breath on my neck makes a chill run up my spine.

"I've got you," he says comfortingly, "I won't let her hurt you."

My eyes widen as the realization sets in that he was the one who knocked me out at the end of that night and that he was the one who whispered in my ear before I fell unconscious.

"Jordan," I whisper, my eyes tearing up, "I can't trust you."

"You can trust me," he whispers back, "I made sure she didn't kill you that night. I told her I ended it, and that was that. I ensured she didn't have a reason to return and finish the job. You need to follow my lead here. Do as I say; I refuse to play her games. She saw you on the trail when you woke up and decided she needed to make sure to end you. She's insane."

My gut tells me to rip myself from his grasp, but my heart tells me something completely different. It's telling me that I can trust him, and unfortunately, I tend to follow what it tells me. I'm still keeping my walls up around him because he's still my psychotic therapist's son, and everything I've learned in therapy has told me that mental problems are genetic. This could be a ploy.

"Okay. I trust you." My lip quivers out of fear, and I attempt to steady it to keep my tone even.

"I trust you with everything I am." I'm unsure if I'm trying to convince him or myself.

Jordan shushes me, and I look ahead, seeing Emma quickly return from the car. She has a few items in her hands, but I can't quite make out what it is in the dark. She walks past us without a word, and Jordan's fake, aggressive demeanor returns. He tightens his grasp on my wrists and turns me around with so much force that my neck cracks.

A few feet ahead of me, I see a massive brush pile filled with leaves and sticks; it's about the size of the bonfire we built the night of the festival. Emma dances around it, and the scent of gasoline fills the air. The sound of sloshing liquid hits the ground. I wiggle, attempting to get out of Jordan's grip, but he grabs my arms tighter than before.

"Stop," he whispers as Emma disappears behind the bonfire pit.

"We need to make this look legitimate if you're really here to help me and not hurt me," I say, turning my head around to get a peak of his expression.

Emma comes back around the front and looks at me with evil eyes. Her smile spreads from ear to ear, and she grits her teeth. She tosses the gas can into the fire pit and backs away, striking a match against the side of a matchbox. Momentarily, her face is illuminated. I am greeted by the true face of evil staring back at me instead of the supposed evil she thinks she is saving the world from.

Emma tosses the match into the fire pit, and instantly, the forest is flooded with light, and the heat causes sweat to immediately bead down my forehead, rolling down the bridge of my nose. She bends down and picks up a knife and a gun that had been placed on the ground. She looks back and forth between the two weapons as if she's deciding which one to use on me.

"Jordan, what do we do?" The question slides past my shaking lips. I know he needs to keep up the facade, but it doesn't look like we have much time to come up with a plan.

"Do you have a plan?" I ask. Jordan, tell me you do."

"I have a plan." I can hear in his tone that he's smiling, "Just trust me."

"It's getting harder to trust you by the second," I chuckle nervously.

"Well, well, well," Emma laughs as she saunters toward us, "Jordy, should we finish her with a knife or a gun?" Her eyes flick between the two in her hands.

"Which one will cause her to suffer longer, Mom?" He asks with a growl.

Mom?

"Hmm. We can get more creative with the knife—make her bleed out slower." Emma states.

"Let's go knife then," Jordan confirms.

I turn back again, and my eyes widen toward him. I wiggle my hands again, but I can't seem to escape his grip. My mind runs a million miles a minute, and my thoughts jump back and forth between trust and distrust.

I don't know what to do.

He holds me tighter against him, and I can feel his chest pushing into my shoulder blades. He rests his chin on my shoulder.

"She's going to go against my choice—she always does. She's going to use the gun. When she raises her arm and points it toward you, I will release you and push you away. Run. Run as fast and far as possible and take this with you." Jordan's words are quick and deliberate. Suddenly, I feel a cold metal handle against the palm of my hand, and he secures my fingers around it.

"I'm going to wrestle the gun from her hands and chase after you. Don't look back. Don't wait for me. Just run. Do you understand me?"

I nod my head as Emma closes the gap between us, holding the knife out and pointing at me with it. I swallow hard, and it feels like a lump in my throat.

Suddenly, she drops her hand holding the blade and raises the other one holding the gun. Jordan's hands loosen around my wrists, and I adjust my stance to push off the ground as hard as possible. She stops before me, and I detect a light shake in her hand. She doesn't want to do this but feels like she needs to.

Because God told her she needed to.

I can't believe that's a sentence I just said to myself.

Emma reaches across herself and pulls back on the slide of the handgun, and Jordan's grip disconnects from my hands.

"Now," he growls in my ear.

I sprint as quickly as I can toward the tree line, and behind me, I hear a gunshot ring through the air. Against Jordan's directions, I stopped and turned to look. Jordan is on the ground, holding his shoulder with Emma by his side. The bullet hit him instead of me, and I couldn't be more thankful for his sacrifice, but at the same time, now I've killed his girlfriend and have maybe killed him, too.

Jordan turns his head and looks in my direction. " Run," he screams, the sound of his voice bouncing off the trees.

I do as I'm told and take off running again into the trees, dodging downed limbs as I do. The woods are just as dark as the night Jordan and I were wandering around. I can't see anything in front of me, and I pat my pockets, realizing my phone is missing, so I can't even use the flashlight.

I find a fallen tree large enough to cover my entire body, and I duck down behind it. My breath is ragged, and I breathe deeply in an attempt to control it. The howling of a coyote can be heard nearby, and I have to close my eyes to focus on my breathing and slow my heart rate down. The pounding in my ears makes it difficult to hear my surroundings.

Suddenly, the sound of footsteps carefully and deliberately walking through the woods catches my ear. I press my back against the tree trunk as hard as possible, flattening myself as much as possible. From the corner of my eye, I catch a figure stepping over the tree I'm hiding behind.

It's now or never.

"Jessica," Emma says my name in a singsongy tone as if attempting to intimidate me.

Using the little light, I have shining down through the trees from the moon, I make my best guess at where her leg is as I clutch the knife Jordan gave me. I take a chance at what I believe to be Emma's heel and stab the blade, trying to hit her Achilles. A scream and a thud later, and Emma is on the ground.

Heaving myself up and over, I clamber over the tree trunk and take off running through the woods again. I should have taken the opportunity and finished the job, but I need to make sure that Jordan is okay. It's my fault that he's injured. I break through the trees and see Jordan lying on the ground.

"Jordan," I scream.

He looks up and slowly lifts himself back up into a sitting position as I run toward him. I reach him and kneel at his side.

"Jordan, I'm so sorry." I begin sobbing hysterically.

"Jess, it's okay. I knew it was going to happen. I prepared for it as I told you what to do. I moved just in time. She hit my shoulder, and the bullet went straight through. I'm going to be fine."

"I-I-I think I cut her Achilles tendon. She went down. What do we do now?" I ask. Tears are streaming down my face uncontrollably.

"Jessica," Jordan says, placing the palms of his hands on my cheeks, "you need to calm down. This next step is crucial."

He places something cold and heavy into my hand. The gun.

"Kill her," he says forcefully.

"B-B-but, Jordan, I can't."

"You need to."

"I've already killed Brielle, I can't kill your mom, too."

"Jess." His tone is stern. "Will you stand by me when this is all over?"

I nod my head.

"Then I don't need her. I don't need Brielle. I need you. Someone who was here. Someone who went through this with me, someone who knows what it was like. I don't care who you've killed or how close I was to them. Especially my mom. She started this. You are going to finish it."

I hear rustling behind me, and I don't have time to argue with Jordan now. Emma is stumbling out of the woods, dragging the leg that I slashed behind her. I look back to Jordan, and he nods his head.

"Do it," he mouths.

Taking in a deep breath, I stand up and turn toward Emma. She's slowly closing the gap between us. I raise my arm and point the gun at her.

"Emma, don't move another inch, or I'll put a bullet between your eyes." My hand is shaking, and I don't sound terribly confident.

She notices it, too, because she keeps walking toward us and lets out a roar of laughter.

"You wouldn't. You don't have it in you," she mocks.

I begin to back away as she is within ten feet of me, and I grab the gun with my other hand, attempting to stabilize myself. She limps around me, and now she is standing next to Jordan. She looks down at him, and he gives her a crooked half-smile. She cocks back and punches him in the face, and blood immediately begins running from his nose, dripping and staining his shirt.

"Disobedient child," she says.

He shoots me a look of approval to do what he's asked me to do.

I manage to steady my hand and begin walking toward Emma.

"I am done with this shit," I announce, "you are not God. You are not God's right-hand man. You are not the chosen one. You may feel all-powerful right now, but soon, you will find that God does not have your back, God cannot save you, and your God has left you to your own devices. This is over, Emma, and if you ask me, you're the evil one here, not all those innocent people you killed. You carried out your own version of a witch hunt, and you did nothing but kill. This is on you; this is not on God. You're nothing more than a psychopath. You need help. You'd think a psychologist could recognize that."

I continue marching forward in her direction, and she stumbles backward, holding the knife out in front of her in an attempt to threaten and intimidate me.

"No matter what happens, God's got me. I am saved. You are not. You will burn for eternity." She is almost backed up entirely to the fire pit. She's got to be feeling the fires of hell burning on her back.

"I'm not the one who will burn. You will. The sixth commandment says, 'Thou shall not kill,' and you have killed. You have tortured and abused." I point to Jordan. "And I'm going to make sure you can never hurt anyone again."

Taking in a deep breath, I squeeze the trigger on the gun, and as the shot goes off, my ears begin to ring, and I squeeze my eyes shut. I'm not sure that I even hit her until I reopen them. I watch as a blood spot spreads across her abdomen, staining through her shirt. I squeeze again, firing another round, and she stumbles backward. I close the distance between us as she falls backward directly into the fire.

Emma begins to scream as the flames encapsulate her being. I stand over her and observe as her skin seemingly melts off her face. Her eyes are wide, and she reaches a hand out toward me. My eyes bore into her soul.

"Burn in hell," I say.

I turn around and run back to Jordan's side as he breathes a sigh of relief. I put an arm around his shoulders, and he winces as I touch the spot where he was shot. We walk back to the car without a word, but the two of us turn around and stare at the fire to ensure that Emma isn't escaping.

With a struggle, Jordan raises a hand and places it on my cheek, making me make eye contact with him. He smiles at me, and I can feel my quickly beating heart melting. He removes his hand and places it out in front of him as if to offer a handshake. I look at him, confused, but place my hand in his.

"I'd like to start over," he begins, "I'm Jordan. Nice to meet you."

"Jessica," I respond.

"Jessica, can I take you out sometime?" He asks.

I chuckle. "You want to take me out, like on a date, or do you want to take me out like she did?"

"On a date," Jordan confirms.

"I'd like that," I reply.

We return to the car, and I help him enter the passenger seat. I walk around the back of the car and slam the still-open trunk closed. I look back at the fire and shake my head. I take a deep breath and exhale slowly, smile, then walk around to the front of the car. I slide into the driver's seat and look at Jordan. He looks back and smiles again as we begin driving away for the last time, never to return to the scene of the festival again.